MEWING

CHLOE SPENCER MEWING

A NOVELLA

Content warnings are available at the back of this book.

Mewing is a work of fiction. The characters, incidents, and dialogue are creations of the author's imagination or are used fictitiously. Any resemblance to actual events or persons, living or dead, is entirely coincidental.

Cover art and interior design by Alan Lastufka.

First Edition published February 2024.

10 9 8 7 6 5 4 3 2 1

ISBN 978-1-959565-21-5 (Paperback)
ISBN 978-1-959565-22-2 (eBook)

To those who stood in front of their mirror with a pair of scissors wishing they could transform every part of themselves.

MEWING

The practice of shaping one's jaw by adjusting the placement of the tongue in the mouth. Typically, one will put their tongue just behind their upper front teeth to achieve the effect of a slimmed jawline. Certain risks are involved with this activity, such as misalignment of the jaw, pain within the jaw, and loose or chipped teeth from the pressure. Those interested in this practice should first consult with their respective doctor, orthodontist, or dentist.

PART ONE

Although Vix had only 30 thousand followers, her latest post of her freshly waxed dewy body in a violet bikini attracted 100 thousand likes—the highest she had ever received. She watched with wide doe eyes as all the little red hearts trickled in, and, with each one, her body felt that much warmer. Soon after came the comments, many of which consisted of compliments from undisciplined horny men or self-shaming teenage girls whining about how ugly they looked in comparison. The brand commented with a series of heart-face emojis, followed by, "Thank you Vixxxxx we <3 you!" Shortly after, they DM'd her an offer to send her more designer swimsuits, shipped straight from their sweatshop factory in northern Morocco.

She accepted them, of course. She had been

eying their one-piece red swimsuit with the plunging neckline for quite a while, but that $175 price tag was too steep for her budget right now. Her pocket-sized studio apartment, high above the streets of DeLongpre Avenue, painfully reminded her of her ever-dwindling bank account. The pathetic strings of LED lights she had hung around the windows and over her kitchen countertop did next to nothing to brighten up the beige space. No matter. There were plenty of places to go—even on a sleepy Wednesday night.

She pushed away her blush-pink sheets and crawled off her queen-sized mattress, then traipsed over to her closet. The doors creaked open, and she inhaled the musty smell from inside. She eyed the speckled black strips that dripped down from the ceiling. They were small and subtle; something too insignificant to worry about but concerning enough to leave a lingering question.

She reached into her closet and removed her best pair of boyfriend jeans, her platform raven-black high tops, and her *va-va-voom* red corset. Was it appropriate to wear out in the streets of down-town Wichita? Nope, but perfectly acceptable here. Encouraged, in fact. And what her mom and Gran didn't know would only make her more desirable to the sleazy wretches who offered pretty, vapid girls modeling contracts.

Only Vix wasn't vapid. She thought of herself, proudly (as in Taylor Swift *Reputation*-era fashion), as a snake. Capable of molting her skin and personality to conform to whatever situation that arose in her pathway to stardom. What that stardom was, she didn't know. Singer, actress, or model—maybe all three. Wherever her fame carried her, she would go with it. She had decided that for herself a long time ago, and despite her mother's desperate pleas to stay in the Midwest, Vix had rejected all desire for a quiet, comfortable life. Come hell or high water, she was going to do what it took to become a star—no matter if she had to beg, borrow, or steal the hearts of thousands of faceless strangers.

She clipped on her silver hoop earrings and examined her look in the mirror. *Almost.* She turned her head from side to side and applied a fresh shade of lipstick to match her vivacious top. After running her tongue over her teeth, she smiled—devilishly sharp and polished.

She was dressed to kill.

* * *

BUBBLES INC. was the boba shop around the corner from where she lived. $15 a cup was a steep price to pay for a drink, but it was worth it for the 'gram. The shop also made their own custom taiyaki, and when she stepped through the door, the smell of sugar-sweet eggy batter filled her nostrils: a direct assault on the low-cal keto diet she had enacted only two weeks before moving to California. Guiltily, she ordered both the taro-flavored drink and the dessert; the chocolate-drizzled matcha flavor satisfied all her cravings. While awaiting her order, she pulled out her phone and pretended to look busy, but really, she was trying to figure out where the best light was in the room.

Damn. Everything in here made her look washed out. The raccoon circles, courtesy of too many late nights drinking diet rosé from Whole Foods, were distinctive in the stark, white lighting. It made her pores—black and stubbly like the insides of her thighs—look bigger. If she had a magnifying glass, she could see inside herself. Speaking of? She made sure no one was watching, and she tried to rub her legs together to scratch them. Apparently a full-on Brazilian was no match for her Italian genes. She felt the prickly little hairs, deep in the recesses of her body, starting to reform. The tiny, phantom red-hot pains drove her attention to the places that would surely develop ingrown hairs.

There go the new bikini pics, she thought.

When her order was called, she retrieved it and sat down. She snapped a few pics on her phone and fussed with the various filters to bring out the colors. She selected a new one—Mania—and applied it to her photo. It was vibrant and highly saturated, and, after she adjusted the contrast, perfectly balanced. She smiled as she pressed upload but couldn't move to eat or sip until the first few hundred likes came in. #foodporn. Always a hit.

Midway through her first bite of delectable ice cream, she heard someone call her name—a familiar voice, fried and high pitched. When Vix turned to look in her direction, she fought to keep the bile from rising in her throat. Josslyn Brooks, her ombré lavender hair freshly blown-out and curled, stared at her from across the small store. She stumbled forward in wedges that were so high she nearly tripped head over heels.

What a shame, Vix thought. *If she fell, she'd break those stupid legs of hers in two.* Long, tan, and not a scar or bruise on them. Sharply chiseled muscles as if carved by Michelangelo himself. No number of hours on a steady bike or lunges could ever give Vix legs half as nice. Her thighs were flaccid, jiggly, and round—they often reminded her of a dead baby pig's torso, if said baby pig had been bleached in the sun for eighteen hours.

"Girl, I thought you were on a diet!" Josslyn chirped, removing her sunglasses.

For the briefest of moments, her eyes scanned over the boba and taiyaki almost longingly. But then she popped a chunk of spearmint gum in her mouth and pulled out her phone instead. Horrified, Vix stared at Josslyn, wishing she would somehow spontaneously combust or get bored and leave. She set down her ice cream sandwich and smiled at her intrusive frenemy.

"How are you, Joss? Still working on getting that payment from the last sponsor?"

Joss looked up. "You mean BeautyMilk? Oh, no. They paid me. You know how invoicing works."

Vix had only ever been paid to work with brands five times and had never once had to worry about invoicing those companies. They all PayPaled her. Josslyn was a same-day-deposit-in-the-bank-account kind of bitch, evident by her name-brand bag and clothes dripping with logos. Holy shit, was that a new Dolce and Gabbana?

Calm. Vix willed herself to maintain patience. *Snake.* She smiled warmly at her.

"I'm so glad to hear that. I've heard some real horror stories."

"You got any sponsorships as of yet?"

"You see the bikini pic I posted earlier today?"

"Oh, from your trip to Long Beach? Yeah."

"They're going to send me more swimsuits in the mail."

Josslyn blinked. "And?"

And? "They wanted me to model them. It's their new collection."

A sigh—and a pang in Vix's chest. Josslyn set her bedazzled phone face down on the table and gently patted her hand. It was so condescending, but her smile was so soft and affectionate. *Snake, snake, snake.*

"Honey. You cannot let these brands take advantage of you. They wanna pimp you out, they gotta pay." She shook her head. "You want to be a model, right? How are you going to build a portfolio without photos from a brand account?"

Wasn't her Insta her portfolio? But that stupid smile said otherwise. Vix's facade faltered. She averted her eyes from Josslyn, and that was when she went in for the kill.

"Have you gotten any modeling opportunities since you moved here? It's been what, three months?"

Three months, nearing four. Vix could only nod, ashamed.

"What kind of numbers are we doing?"

"30K on Insta, maybe 10K on TikTok. About 5K on Twitter." Twitter was always challenging, since it was the place where she had to be the most outraged to gain any kind of traction. Negative engagement went farther there, and that conflicted with her carefully curated TikTok and Insta personas that centered on sweetness and sexiness.

Josslyn winced and sucked in air through her teeth. "Ooh. Sweetie, there is no reason why you shouldn't be pulling in those sponsos. You gotta put yourself out there."

Vix caved. It was no use. Josslyn smelled the weakness in her game like blood to a shark. She picked up her sandwich again for comfort. "I've been trying, but no bites."

"Oh honey. And you're renting that place around the corner from here, right?" A series of tongue clicks. *Tut, tut, tut.* Ramming the shame in even harder. "You're doing alright for yourself? I mean, I'm assuming you're living off ramen like we all do when we first move here, but please tell me you've at least got running water and aren't, like, burning candles so you can see at night."

"Uh. . . I mean, I'm doing social media for Firestorm Games. So that gets me by okay." That was a complete lie. The job only paid her $15 an hour and offered her, at most, 10 hours a week. She was burning through her savings faster than the Catholic Church had blown through the Holy Land during the Crusades. "But. . . I would love any kind of job. Modeling or otherwise."

Josslyn's Tiffany Blue eyes widened. She looked around the shop, as if to make sure the bored teenager working at the counter wasn't listening. Then she reached across, grabbed a napkin, and using a pen from her purse, wrote down a social media handle.

"Insta?"

Josslyn shook her head. "Twitter. You gotta DM them first." She pushed the napkin over to her. "You heard of influencer houses, right?"

"B-but Joss, I already have a place to live."

"I know, I know. But it's like. . . like a guild! Like SAG, but more casual and family-like. You get in, and they hook you up. I think you gotta sign a contract or some shit, but after like, a certain number of months, you're free to go if you want."

"What do they do?"

"Girl." Josslyn smiled. "They hook. You. *Up*. This house is called Bleach Babes. Y'know. Cause they're all bleach blonde?"

Vix could not bring herself to laugh at the joke that was barely a joke. "So? Jobs? Gigs?"

"Yeah. And they live in a house in the hills. Now, it's not a mansion, but it's in a gated community, so it's pretty sweet digs. I mean, this is Insta money, not Emmy award-winning actress money. But you could do well for yourself. *Hook-ups*."

She clapped her hands together to emphasize the last two words. The ice cream sandwich in Vix's hands dripped green goodness onto the steel table below. Josslyn wrinkled her nose and tousled her hair.

"You might want to cut back on the sweets if you're going to be a model, babe."

That night Vix dumped the rest of her boba tea down the toilet. The black tapioca pearls, like little ships in a storm, struggled against the crashing waves as they were sucked down the drain.

* * *

One quick Google search brought up tens of thousands of search results for the Bleach Babes. Magazine covers, ET spotlights, and carefully curated Instagram stories all made Vix's heart flutter with excitement. Josslyn may be a bitch, but she was at least a smart bitch. As Vix scrolled through the first page of results, she found something interesting: #LeilaniLost. She opened the hashtag on Twitter and was flooded with a series of pleas for information, cries for help, and photos of a sun-kissed girl laying across a bed, a coy smile on her face. Indie musician and songwriter Leilani Laurenta, a member of the Bleach Babes who, at the time of her disappearance, had just become the newest member of a now defunct all-girl pop group. The missing persons investigations case for her had closed almost a year ago. For a brief second, Vix felt a twinge of danger, but oddly enough, she found it more alluring than worthy of anxiety. Rich, hot, and a sense of mystery? These girls were *it.* They were the missing factor to her online persona, to the entire trajectory of her career.

A series of Twitter DMs later, Vix had the address of the house. She dressed in her model finest: a black bodysuit, paired with black jeans in a slightly different shade, and her tallest black boots. She had learned from a blog long ago that this sort of outfit would make her appear slimmer and taller. Far too nervous to drive, she ordered an Uber, although her credit card alerts aggressively warned her that she was inching closer to her limit. *Ping, ping, ping, you broke ass bitch.* Spending thirty bucks on a drive when she already had her little 2005 Honda Accord but didn't want people to know how shitty it was. No. She had to be glamorous. Modelesque. To become the snake.

The Uber driver's name was Mohamed, and he greeted her with a bright smile even when she did not acknowledge his presence. She slid into the backseat of his Pacifica Chrysler and buckled up, then turned her attention to her phone. She was well-aware that he kept staring at her in her rearview, although she did not look back at him. She only glanced up once—to look out the window when the car started climbing the steep hill that led to the gated community. The gate itself was constructed with immaculately shaped bricks in every shade of red imaginable.

"I'm sorry," he said. He had bright white teeth, but a gap-toothed smile—the kind that looked good on rich British girls with fake freckles and dyed-red hair. In another life, he could've been in a toothpaste commercial. "I'm surprised you're dressed in all black in this weather."

Vix smiled politely. "Yeah. I might have a modeling gig."

"Oh, that's exciting." He tapped his fingers on the steering wheel. "A model. Crazy the kind of people you meet in this city, honestly. Y'know, last night, I kid you not, I drove home the singer of that new band. Y'know, the one with the hit single? They won't stop playing it."

Vix didn't listen to the radio, and embarrassingly, stuck strictly to her curated Spotify playlist. But she played along. "What band?"

"Uhh. . . I think it was Traveling Earls. Something like that. They have the song, *Need to Forget You?* Something like that. It was originally written by that girl. . . Layla or something." He drummed his hands on the steering wheel and sang-hummed the tune with a deep, soulful vibrato.

I need to forget you
But I don't know how
It feels like every time I turn around
You're right there staring back at me
And even though I want to, I can't leave
I need to forget you
But I don't know why
Each step I take, I want to die
Torn apart inside

When he finished, he stared at Vix in the rearview mirror, waiting for her approval. She gave a polite smile, and he launched into a detailed explanation of the night's events, talking about how he picked up the band from this-and-that club, took them to In-and-Out, etcetera, etcetera, etcetera. It was clear he was lying, and poorly at that, but Vix continued to indulge him. Asked questions about his star-studded encounter. Was sweet. Then slowly pretended to have more pressing engagements on her phone until he got the hint.

He did say one more thing though, just before she got out of the car. "Have I seen you somewhere before?"

"Me?"

"Yeah. Are you an actress?" Smiling again. "I only ask because my daughter Zahara likes it if I bring her autographs."

"Well, maybe one day if I end up an actress, I can give her one."

And with that, she shut the door and walked away. She pulled up her phone and opened her app, questioning whether or not to leave a poor review. But the sight in front of her was too distracting to concern herself with such petty things.

The house sat upon the crest of the hill, nestled comfortably between two other equally large houses. The driveways were lined with cobblestones, the roofs a red Spanish tile, twinkling bright in the heat of the California sun. Mission style architecture with trimming a dark mahogany rich and red like Vix's chipping nail polish. *Wait*. Chipping? *Oh shit*. Dread rose in her chest as she approached the house's front door, moseying past a sparkling clean silver Maserati. That's what she had missed. *Stupid, stupid, stupid*. She had failed her mission before she had even knocked.

But she was the snake, and the snake could camouflage. She knocked on the door and folded her hands against her body. She scrubbed away the polish with her nails and pushed back her cuticles with ferocious strength, rendering them red and raw. After a few moments, the door opened, and behind it stood a young woman with trademark bleach blonde hair. In her other hand she held a DSLR on a gimbal. She was pretty, with sharp cheekbones. A long Grecian nose in the center of a perfectly symmetrical face. Bleach Babe number one: Iona Stathopoulos. Spiritual yoga instructor and self-proclaimed wellness mentor. Two hundred fifty thousand followers on Insta.

"Name?"

"Vix," she said. "I'm like, so excited to meet you."

A smile crinkled across her face. "Like, totally. You're supposed to meet with Margo, right?"

"Yeah."

"Cool, I'll go get her." Iona did not move but turned her body three quarters towards the stairs and then shouted at the top of her lungs, "Margo! She's here!"

A pause. Iona sighed, as if she had expected Margo to appear instantaneously, and since she hadn't, it was a profound disappointment. She shook her head and stepped back, allowing Vix to enter.

"Shoes." Iona snapped her fingers and pointed at Vix to take off her boots.

Vix bent down and tried to unzip them, but these were nearly thigh-high, and they also had a thick platform base. She looked up to ask Iona for a chair, but the girl was gone, bouncing off to another section of the house. Vix shut the front door behind her and with heated cheeks, sat on the floor so that she could take them off. But the zipper stuck on the leg of her pants, and try as she might to wrestle with it, it wouldn't come loose. She gritted her teeth and pulled, her little speckled nails digging into the mesh of the zipper, and with a furious cry, she ripped it free.

"She told you to take your boots off, didn't she?"

The woman spoke in a low, molasses-rich voice. Vix looked up with wide eyes. Another bleach blonde, older than she was but with a perfectly sculpted body, and eyes even bluer than Josslyn's. Her lips, plump with filler, formed a pouty, sultry smile. The woman wore a white maxi dress with spaghetti thin straps. Her collarbone was immaculately smooth, and her cleavage was tasteful but not slutty. This was *her*. The one with over three million followers. The one who was on the cover of *Vogue Sweden*, was the Cover Girl of the Year 2011, was ranked number sixteen on the Top Fifty Most Fashionable in Hollywood. The only daughter of the late Astrid Nilsson, famous supermodel extraordinaire.

Margo Eriksen.

She pushed back a strand of her hair and tucked it behind her ear, patiently yet impatiently waiting for Vix to finish taking off her boots. Vix did, feeling rushed and embarrassed. She scrambled to her feet and stuck out her trembling hand. Margo looked down. Vix winced.

"V-Vixen Morello. Margo, it's such an honor to meet you."

Margo gazed intensely at her for another

moment. It made Vix want to throw up. But then the sugarcoated smile returned, and soon she felt the heat of Margo's palm against her own. *And the texture.* By God, this woman had hands as smooth as polished glass, and fingernails just as sharp and shiny and healthy. What kind of vitamins was she taking?

"Pleasure to meet you, Vix. Thank you so much for reaching out." She looked over her shoulder, presumably in the direction that Iona had gone. She spoke in a hushed murmur, soothing yet serious. "You'd never know this about her, but she's a little OCD. If she lets you in the house, she makes you take off your shoes. Anyway, why don't we go into my office to chat?"

Margo's office was a massive room, at least twice the size of Vix's whole apartment. Massive floor to ceiling bay windows allowed ample sunlight to trickle in. A wall divided the space in half, separating a small series of bookshelves from the desk and ring light on the other side. A lonely tripod, pointed at the office chair, waited for its camera. But most peculiar was the artwork, hanging on the wall behind the desk: a lineless, abstract work of a bleached deer skull, its antlers protruding long and proud. It seemed vaguely macabre in nature, almost out of place for the office, but at least adhered to the color palette of the overall space.

Vix took a seat in the egg-shaped chair across from the desk. She sunk down so low, she thought she would fall through, and she scrambled to adjust her posture. Margo noticed. Small smile. Curious arch of her freshly threaded brow. She sat down and opened her phone.

"So. . . Wichita, right?"

"Yes."

"I'm a Minnesota girl myself. Though you probably could've guessed."

"Oh, I wouldn't have. . . uh, known. You don't do the thing with the *o's*. You know?" Vix laughed. *"Dontcha know?"*

Margo blinked, unamused. "We don't talk like that. I meant that I'm Scandinavian. I'm assuming you know I was on the cover of *Vogue Sweden*?"

"O-oh! Yes! I've. . . been a follower of yours for a long time."

That was a lie. Vix had only learned about her after her Google search, and further, she had only recognized Margo because she was Astrid's daughter. If Margo called her on her bluff, she could always claim that she was following her on her alt account. Then again, would Margo have noticed one measly follower out of the three million she had? Did she have some sort of vetting process that would've double-checked for that sort of thing?

"That's lovely. Always nice to meet a fan. So you told me you want to break into modeling? Is that really what you want to do?"

"Y-yeah, honestly. I'm down to do anything. I have gotten a few requests from brands to cover their stuff, but none have paid me so far. And my friend Joss said that was common, but. . . I don't know. I'm not getting any modeling jobs or paid for any brand requests." Vix shrugged her shoulders and shook her head. "That's why I'm so excited for this opportunity with you. I mean, you're so talented. You built an empire from scratch, busted your butt to get where you are—"

Margo hung her head and held up her hand. "Stop."

Vix stared. Margo raised her head to meet her gaze, unimpressed.

"I can tell you," she said, "exactly what your problem is."

Vix leaned closer.

"You're fawning. Do you know what fawning is?" Margo propped her chin up on her hand.

"Uh. . ." Vix trailed off nervously. "I don't. . ."

"Fawning is when you try too hard to be nice to someone. Happens when you perceive someone as a threat. It's what you're doing now, and you do *not* do that to me." She leaned back in her seat and folded her arms, appraising her. "I invited you into my home to help you, and because I saw your potential. So don't you dare walk in here and think you can throw yourself at my feet to get in my good graces, then later gossip about me to get ahead like a passive aggressive little shitheel. I've been doing this for years, I can see right through it, and so can others. It's pathetic, and it's why people will either not like you or take advantage of you." She took a deep breath. "So let's start over. Who are you really, Vixen Morello?"

Vix shook her head. "Just a girl from Wichita."

Margo snapped her fingers and pointed at her, like she was a dog who shat on the carpet. "I'm warning you."

"But really! That's who I am."

"Who are you, Judy fucking Garland? I can't sell *Wichita*." She spoke the word in a hiss, as if it was a curse. "You know what girls from Wichita get? Put on the varsity cheer squad, knocked up by their high school boyfriend, and forced to fuck a stupid man for the rest of their lives so they can keep the lights on and get their T. J. Maxx credit cards paid. So tell me Vix, is that you?"

"If you're asking me if I fuck stupid men, then yeah. Sometimes I do," Vix replied. Gone was the vocal fry and sugar-cookie voice. Her eyebrows rose. *Rude.* She clapped a hand over her mouth, but Margo smiled and nodded her approval.

"And why?" Margo asked, leaning closer to her. "Why do you fuck stupid men?"

Vix swallowed. The framed front covers of magazines, each with a different Bleach Babe, seemed to stare back at her menacingly. Knowingly. The variety of colors of outfits, some pastel, others neon and springy, seemed to bleed and blend together on the wall behind Margo, like a nauseating kaleidoscope. She recognized Leilani's face, beaming and bright and full of life. But even the reminder of a missing girl paled in comparison to the most intense object on the wall: the deer skull painting. Although it didn't have eyes like the models, it seemed to stare right into her soul, filling her with a sense of deep dread, but somehow, still anchoring her in place, as if bewitching her. She kept her eyes on the painting as she spoke.

"Because I like having that control—I like the power that comes with knowing I'm smarter than them. And because stupid men plow you better. Smart guys overthink everything when they fuck you." Vix folded her arms and stared at the floor, deep in thought. "The last smart dude I tried to fuck overthought everything so much he scared himself impotent. But on the bright side, smart guys will have all the money to pay for dinner. So you gotta fuck both types of dudes to keep a balance."

Margo clapped for her. And Vix felt proud. A heated blush blossomed across her cheeks.

"That's the kind of honesty I expect from you if we're going to work together. You give me honesty, and I'll give you honesty in return." Margo reached into her desk and withdrew a menthol cigarette. Vix's eyebrows rose, deeply surprised. She knew plenty of people who vaped, but not cigarettes. "May I?" Vix nodded, and Margo outstretched her hand, gesturing to her phone. Vix unlocked it and placed it in her grasp. Margo proceeded to swipe through. "So, rundown of your accounts. Twitter, Insta, TikTok?"

"Yep. Trying to get more active on TikTok."

"You gotta be good at it to be on TikTok. Are you funny? You write good jokes? Do cute dances?"

Vix winced. "I mostly stitch things and react to stories."

"Meh. Skip it then. You got anything else I should know about? Secret *Twilight* stan YouTube account from when you were ten? Poorly written fanfiction on *Supernatural's* AO3? An OnlyFans?"

Vix bit her lip. "No YouTube. Made an OnlyFans once to see if I could sell some pics of my feet for cash but it didn't... pan out. I deleted it."

"You deleted it?" Margo puffed on her cigarette and blew a cool cloud of minty smoke into the air.

She nodded. "Yeah. Deleted it. And it was never linked to my other socials. Like I said, it was a cash grab. And all I ended up grabbing were creepy messages from 40-year-old men with sunglasses holding fish in their profile pic."

"It's fine if you still have one. Francesca—she's a member of the house but doesn't live here for obvious reasons—she's an adult film star and model. The reason why I ask these things is so that I can figure out how to work your image." Margo smirked. "So I guess porn is out of the question for you?"

Vix seriously considered this. "I mean..."

"If you wanted to do it, you would say yes right

away. You don't, so that's fine." Margo squashed the smoking end of her barely-touched cigarette into her pink ashtray. "You look a little confused dear, so why don't I pass the floor to you? Ask me anything."

"Um. . ." Vix fidgeted in her seat. "Joss didn't really tell me anything about. . . what you guys do. Are you an agent? A manager?"

"One could say I'm a manager, although for legal and personal reasons, I prefer not to use that word," Margo replied. "Agents come with a lot of regulations within the entertainment industry, managers less so. I prefer to think of myself as a career mentor. I found that by doing that, as opposed to providing representation, I've been able to have healthier professional relationships."

Her calculative phrasing scarcely registered to Vix, who was entranced by both Margo's beauty and her blunt professionalism. "I started the Bleach Babes in 2018 after I made *Vogue*. I realized that collabs, as I'm sure you know, do well for numbers and engagement. So I figured, what better way than to put all of us in a house together? At first it was only the five of us, and then less, and then some more, and then finally it grew into this. . . community. Not all of us live here of course, but many did at one point."

"Oh, well I have an apartment. But um, it *is* a month-to-month lease, so. . ."

"Well, it's all dependent on how serious you

want to take it. You want to do modeling exclu-
sively? How big do you want to be?"

"Like. . . ?"

"The modeling world is a lot bigger than it feels,
Vix. You've got your high fashion—people like me."
As if it wasn't obvious by her pristine features and
envious legs. "And then you've got your commercial
—the girls who show up on the *H&M* ads. And then
you've got the weird ones, and then the just-about-
everything-in-between ones: teeth, hand, skin. It's a
big, big world."

"I'm too short to be a fashion model, but I could
definitely do. . . commercials. I would love that."

Margo nodded. "And that fits with this brand
you're pushing for yourself, right? Wichita-Girl-
Turned-Big-Beauty-Star?"

"I didn't realize until now that was my brand."
Vix blushed again. The way that Margo stared at her
so knowingly made her feel naked. It stirred something uncertain and frightening, yet intoxicating,
inside of her. "I guess you could say I built my
persona based off of what I thought people wanted."

"Ahh. So you think of yourself as a social
chameleon?"

A smirk tugged at the corner of her lips. "I think
of myself as a snake. Because they can shed their
skin and become something brand new."

It felt so strange to admit this to someone else
out loud. But Margo's eyes sparkled, and she nodded
like she appreciated her honesty.

"I'm glad you told me that. That's certainly. . . beneficial. But as you can tell, it runs you into some problems. You're a smart girl, clearly, but you think *too* far ahead, and think too much about others. If you're going to be in the modeling world, you need to be less of a people pleaser. True fashion icons set trends. If you bow to everyone's interests, then you will lose your sense of self. And you won't make it." She drummed her fingertips against the desk. "You have potential, and you need my help. But I need to see more to make this work."

She reached into a filing cabinet behind her, and pulled out a fresh, crisp NDA. She slid it across the table for Vix to sign, along with a glittery pink pen. Gingerly Vix picked up the pen, but she hesitated to put it on the paper. The legalese was printed in a bold, black, and Gothic font—regal, intimidating, and far beyond Vix's reading comprehension skills.

"This is a standard agreement. This isn't your contract," Margo assured her. "Trust me, you're going to have to sign more of these in your career. Best time to start is now."

With a flourish, Vix signed her name. Margo nodded and folded her hands neatly in her lap.

"Come with me."

Margo led Vix up into her room, which was in the west wing of the house. It was gorgeous, with white wainscoting that looked like it had been freshly polished, and a bright, sky blue wallpaper pasted above. From the size of it, the fluffy carpeting, and the presence of the chandelier overhead, it was the master bedroom. Vix barely had a chance to absorb the grand nature of the space before she was escorted to the massive walk-in closet. It had smooth tile on the floors, and crisp white walls like fresh snow. When Margo flicked on the lights everything seemed to sparkle. Each wall was full of clothes, from casual everyday wear to the most gorgeous designer gowns Vix had only ever seen on TV. She had to resist touching each of their sequins and Swarovski crystals as she walked past.

There were no windows in the closet, but there was a massive wall of mirrors, and in the center, one of those giant cushions you'd find to sit on in a shoe store, but posher and upholstered in paisley pink suede. Margo promptly took a seat in front of the mirrors, and Vix quickly tried to sit beside her, but Margo held up her hand.

"Nope. I have to see what I'm working with."

Confused, Vix stared back at her. She laughed, but the seriousness of Margo's expression didn't change. Vix looked at their reflections, and she could see how pale she looked in comparison to Margo's rich, Mediterranean spray tan. She shuffled in place uncomfortably.

"I know it's hard, but I have to do it." She held up her hands. "No cameras. No phones. You're free to inspect every inch of this room if you'd like. But I can assure you, everyone here has had to do this before." She shrugged. "Besides, this isn't the first time you've undressed in front of a woman, is it? You have *nothing* I haven't seen before."

"If that's the case, uh, why strip?" Vix asked. She hated how meager and hoarse her voice sounded—squeaky like a mouse.

"Body type. Figuring out how to dress you." Margo blinked. "Again, you can inspect the space if you'd like, but you've nothing to be afraid of."

"Um. . . is the door locked?"

Margo stood up and exited the space. For a moment, panic filled Vix's body—*You fucking child, you offended her, she hates you, you'll never make it now* —but then she heard the soft shutting of a door, and the faint tumble of a lock. Margo then reentered, shut the door, and locked that door as well.

"I want you to be comfortable, Vix. Please take your time."

But as Margo took her seat again, Vix found herself fumbling with the top button of her jeans. Her whole body radiated heat, but she couldn't tell why she was warm—was it all the damn lights overhead? She slowly unzipped and wriggled her jeans off, then kicked them to the side. She looked at Margo.

"Everything off."

Beet red, Vix reached between her thighs and unclipped her body suit. She pulled it off over her head. Now clad in only her underwear, she looked at

Margo once again, her chest tight, her stomach fluttery.

Her reply was simple: "Off."

Vix closed her eyes and unhooked her black Victoria's Secret bra, then tossed it on top of her pants. She pinched the edges of her bikini underwear and slowly shimmied them down her hips and legs. She turned around, too embarrassed to see Margo's face, but also, too embarrassed to see herself. Jesus, her thighs. She looked like a whale from the waist down. Not to mention, a little bloated, and her breasts small and unimpressive. A pang hit her. Was this Margo's fucked up way of telling her she didn't have the body to be a model? She looked at Margo's reflection, silently begging her to say anything. Margo stood up and faced her. She held up her hands.

"May I?"

Vix nodded, although she was perplexed. Margo's touch was gentle and soft against her skin. She wasn't being assaulted by any means. Part of it felt good—embarrassingly good. This was the fastest she had taken off her clothes for anyone who wasn't a doctor. Margo examined her breasts, pressing two fingers against the soft flesh, and cupping them in her hands. She crouched down low, her face precariously close to Vix's thighs, and poked and prodded at the cellulite there. She looked up at Vix, her expression frank but neutral.

"This is normal," she assured her. "Ninety-five

percent of women have cellulite. This just means we have to put you in the right kind of lighting." She pointed at the ceiling. "If you think you look like shit? It's because of the lighting. These are bright white lights, and you need something with a warmer tone to hide these dimples. But otherwise, good. Thick thighs are in-style, both in commercial and lingerie modeling."

Somehow, Vix felt relieved. Someone liked her ugly, chunky thighs. Said they were on trend and perfect for her career. It made her head a little hazy. When Margo twirled her around to look at her ass, she eagerly complied. Margo glanced at her reflection.

"Nice silhouette. See how your back curves?" she said, pointing at the mirror. "That's gorgeous. A photographer could do a lot with that. Now, your ass though? We gotta pump that up."

"I'm all in for a bigger ass. But do you mean I need surgery?"

Margo shook her head. "Nothing that extreme. It's not like you have nothing to work with. Some girls have walked in here flatter than a pancake. However, there are some other things here and there we might consider later on down the line. Now. . ." Margo pointed to the cushion. "Lay down for me."

The nervousness crept up in the back of Vix's throat, but she obeyed. When Margo pushed apart her trembling legs, she said nothing. She felt the tips of Margo's fingers gingerly press down on the insides of her thighs, and she gritted her teeth. There was no way she was going to start *moaning* after one measly caress. Besides, it wasn't even *meant* to be a caress. Margo was examining her, her brows tightly furrowed.

"You've got some obvious ingrown hairs from this wax. When did you have it done?"

"Uh. . ." Vix trailed off. "I think. . . maybe a week ago?"

"Hmm. Whoever you went to did a sloppy job. Some of the hairs didn't even get removed. We'll need to send you to my esthetician. You can't do bikini pics like this. Not to mention, it clearly hurts like hell. Doesn't it?"

"Like a bitch."

"I'll give you something to put on it before you go. But that's all for the examination." Margo walked over to a section of her clothes and proceeded to peruse her outfits. Vix sat up, her arms folded across her chest. "Let's get you something to wear."

"Wear? O-oh, I. . ."

"We have to find your brand, so we have to find your style. Now today, you're going to have to make a couple of choices. One is whether or not you want to sign with me. And two is who you want to be. Do you really want to go the rest of your life pretending to be Ms. Goody-Goody from Kansas?"

Vix shook her head. "No."

"Right. So that means no pastels, no Peter Pan collars, no gingham, and no flowers."

"*No* flowers?" It wasn't like her entire wardrobe was made up of flower prints, but still. That was going to be pretty hard to part with.

Margo held up a finger. "These are guidelines, not hard and fast rules. Except for the pastels. You don't need to look whiter than you already are. Any shade lighter and I swear to God you'll disappear from existence."

Vix's cheeks blushed pink. "I work indoors."

"You don't need to tell me that. Your body shows it." Margo held up a tight ruched dress against Vix's skin. "You can find out a lot of things about a person from looking at their body."

"You can?"

"Sure. Eating and exercise habits, obviously. Age is another one. But scars and stretchmarks tell so many more delicious stories. They can help you find out what makes a person tick." Margo held up a pair of strappy heels, encouraging Vix to try them on. "All things I'll teach you about in time."

She allowed Margo to dress her like a doll. Swapped out dress after dress, jacket after jacket, blouse after blouse. They opened up jewelry box after jewelry box to find pieces to accent each and every look—and each look was impeccable. Vix had never worn so many nice clothes. The Ethiopian cashmere sweater she pulled over her head for the fifth outfit was soft and smooth like melted butter in a nonstick pan.

"So. . ." Margo said as she folded up some of the clothes. "Vixen. Interesting name. A little devilish for a good Christian girl from the Midwest."

"My dad named me that." Vix laughed. She examined the diamond studded gold chain necklace she wore with high fascination. "The story goes that my mom was too—well—high on the epidural. And my dad thought it would be funny to name me something tangentially related to the holiday."

"You were born on Christmas?"

Vix nodded. "Christmas Eve, yeah. My dad had a bit too much to drink at the family Christmas party, and no one else was there to stop him. Apparently my grandma blew out a tire on the highway, so she was hours late to the hospital."

"And your mother?"

"Mom just. . ." Vix shrugged. "Mom was so out of it. From what she tells me, my birth was really. . . *bad*. They were preparing to go to Midnight Mass, and her water broke outside the church when they were walking by the Nativity scene. And it was so sudden and painful she barely had time to react. She was having contractions as they loaded her into the ambulance."

Margo touched a hand to her chest. "My God."

"She jokes that I had the fear of God in me before I even came out of the womb."

Margo smiled politely. "I think a lot of us do."

"True," Vix said, chuckling. "When she came to the next day, she was of course upset. She started shouting at the nurses and they threatened to send her to the psych ward, she was so hysterical. And eventually she was so busy taking care of me that she didn't have time to be angry about it anymore, much less march her ass down to whatever government office she needed to in order to get it changed."

"Your parents have since divorced, I'm assuming?"

"Y-yeah." Vix was surprised that Margo intrinsically knew this, but then she realized that after the story she just told, it wasn't that surprising to come to that conclusion. "When I was six. I rarely see my dad anymore. And I kinda like it that way."

"Why?"

"Well. . ." Vix twirled around, examining her figure in the mirror. She arched her back in the way that Margo showed her to. "I mean, why else do women not talk to their fathers? He's a self-important asshat who thinks he's so much smarter than anyone with a vagina. And when I started my Insta, he kept making jokes about how I was an attention whore."

"And yet, he named you Vixen."

Vix laughed nervously. "So you're saying he's right?"

Margo shook her head and folded her arms. "I'm saying *he* wanted the attention first. You don't name your daughter Vixen by accident, drunk or sober. He knew exactly what he was doing. I know that type of man well."

"Is your father the same way?"

Margo stood behind Vix and combed her fingers through her hair. She placed her chin on her shoulder. Vix was surprised by how sweet her breath smelled—like the mint smoke from her cigarettes, but also faint traces of caramel, like she just drank a Starbucks Frappuccino.

"He *was*. He was the ambassador to Sweden. Married my mother, who I'm sure you know, was a former pageant queen, in the running for Miss Universe twice—all that good stuff. Men act like women only want attention, but they do too. Otherwise, why would they marry trophy wives? Why marry someone so beautiful that everyone can't help but look at her and want her too? That's not done from love, Vix. That's done from pride." Margo wrapped her arms around her waist, a smile on her lips. "It's so much easier to lie and say you don't want the attention when you do. That's what makes women like us brave. We aren't afraid to admit, out loud, that we want what everyone else wants. It's what made my mother successful, and her mother before her too. An unabashed, unrelenting pursuit of desire."

Vix felt like her skin was burning from Margo's touch. The tingly feeling rose up in her stomach again, and she hoped that Margo couldn't smell the lust leaking from her body. She felt disgustingly damp, and yet, that disgust did nothing to quell her desires. In fact, it made them worse. She gulped and watched as a visible lump slowly dropped down her throat. Margo noticed—her eyes examined the tremors coursing through her body—but then again, as she had learned, Margo noticed everything. Margo tilted her head, her lips nearly pressed against her ear. Vix's body shuddered.

"And you're very brave to be as polite as you have been," Margo murmured, her voice ever so seductive. She giggled, but it wasn't girlish—it was low and dominating. Vix's stomach somersaulted over itself, and as the desire constricted her lungs, she had to open her mouth to let the air in. "I think it's about time you've had a little reward, yeah?" Four sharp eyes, two blue, two brown, staring at their reflections in the mirror. It felt so hot in the room that it looked like their images were wavering, water ripples in the fabric of reality. "What do you think, Vix? Would you like your reward?"

Her first answer came out as a breathless squeak. Margo's grip around her waist tightened.

"No, Vix. Assertive."

She swallowed, and this time when she spoke, she did so with conviction.

"Touch me."

* * *

Panting, Vix laid in a puddle of sweat and secretion on the soft cushion. Margo, who hadn't stripped down at all, stood up and began to tidy the space. Blissfully, Vix remained there, and only her eyes were able to move, watching Margo as she started to put away the jewelry boxes.

"It's been a while," Margo commented, "since I've had someone with so much potential. You might be good enough to be my apprentice."

Vix couldn't respond. Her body was still trembling uncontrollably, her muscles aching from the aftermath of the experience. Her fingers and toes twitched, and she tried her damnedest to regain feeling in them.

"You'll have to dye your hair blonde; I hope you know that. You have a lovely shade of auburn, and it would be a shame to lose it, but we have a brand to maintain. Luckily, we don't have any size requirements. Well." Margo paused. "We have a handful of plus sized models in our midst, but they're no bigger than size fourteens. So I guess you could say that's the maximum—but really, I'm more interested in enforcing the sharp hourglass figure. No pear shapes or rectangles. You have to stick to the diet and exercise regimen that the house nutritionist prepares for you."

"Is that Iona's job?"

Margo's nose crinkled distastefully. "Oh no, honey. You think she knows what she's talking about? No, we have a board-certified nutritionist on staff. Dr. Akonoye. She's quite good at what she does. Of course, you won't get to work with her until you've signed the contract."

Oh right. The contract. In the midst of all of this, Vix had forgotten what she came here for.

"What... are the terms?" She took a deep breath, and that finally gave her the energy she needed to sit up.

"Since you are new, you start off relatively restricted. You are required to present us with copies of your bills and monthly expenditures—receipts will do. None of the money goes directly into your bank accounts. We like to take stock of each girl's value and provide that information to one of our consultants. He basically chooses what stocks to invest in. So essentially, any money you earn goes directly to the house, and I pay for anything you need."

"You... want access to my bank accounts?"

"Not just access. Total control. We need a total accounting of all your assets. Again, this is what helps our financial consultant determine how to invest."

"Invest? In what?"

Margo placed a hand against her cheek, and Vix couldn't help but lean into her touch. "You think we can all look this beautiful forever? Eventually the modeling careers will end for some of us, but it doesn't mean we have to stop living our lifestyle. So yes: in the short term, we maintain your bank accounts. But that's so that we can give you the most financial freedom in the long run."

"How long will you control them?"

Margo shrugged. "Depends. I'm afraid I can't say or explain more unless you're ready to commit. You'll have to sign the contract."

Vix stared down at the ground, trying to consider this. If a man had approached her and told her this, she would've run screaming. But Margo was a businesswoman, well-established and knowl-edgeable about the rules of this game. This was different, wasn't it?

"Another thing, Vix. You said your apartment was month-to-month. Is that correct?"

Vix nodded.

"If you want to be my apprentice, you'll have to move here. But that depends on how far you want to go."

"You'll still pay my rent, even if I decide not to be your apprentice?"

Margo nodded.

"And how many jobs would I need to do? To stay a part of the collective? What sort of restrictions apply to my social media posts? Am I allowed to date?"

Margo smiled. "You don't need to perform any specific number of jobs to be a part of the collective. What you earn belongs to us and is to be shared amongst us. No restrictions on social media, although, if you decide you'd like to try selling your feet again, I would appreciate the heads up for our publicist. And dating? Some restrictions. No one with a low follower count or who is otherwise unworthy." Margo's fingers combed through her hair. "After all, I need to make sure all my girls are well cared for."

She stared at her intently, and Vix couldn't help but be mesmerized by her beauty, her prowess, her confidence. She was everything Vix wasn't but wanted to be. Even though a small part of her subconscious, still drowning in the overwhelming feelings of lust, begged her to listen to reason, she gave it no attention.

Less than a week later, Vix had moved into the Bleach Babe house.

* * *

Her first week there was exhilarating, to say the least. They put her up in a room on the south side of the house, overlooking the pool below. She could catch a glimpse of the Hollywood skyline from her window if she tilted her head at a certain angle. The morning after she moved in, Margo whisked her to a salon, and they chemically drained the color from her hair, leaving it near stark white. The new color complimented Margo's sunnier, fuller color quite well when they stood together, and she loved it for that.

She's the sun, and I am the moon. Vix snapped a

selfie, but Margo intercepted her before she could post it.

"No darling. Like this." She held up Vix's phone, pressed herself against her side, and snapped a pic of them before passing it back to her.

Vix held her phone like it was radioactive. That one pic held untold amounts of social capital. Margo nodded. Vix bit her lip and uploaded it—

—and in minutes, her follower count climbed from thirty thousand to upwards of three hundred fifty thousand. The swollen red hearts filled up her phone so fast it rendered her screen frozen. It vibrated rapidly, and then eventually, stopped making any noise whatsoever—the device simply couldn't keep up. Within minutes, it overheated and died. While Vix stood there trembling, Margo smiled and put on her sunglasses.

"Lucky for you, I have an open spot on my family plan."

After buying a new phone and a quick lunch at an expensive sushi restaurant called Se7en ("Like the film?" Vix had asked, but Margo didn't know), they returned home to answer the numerous phone calls and emails blowing up their accounts. All their followers wanted to know: when were Vix and Margo going to collab? And the brands—"Margo, where have you been hiding this girl until now, and would she like to do a shoot with us?" Margo handled everything, and Vix was grateful for that. She watched as her mentor responded to the potential business collaborators, setting up appointments left and right, and negotiating rates and contracts. Each one Margo tallied up on her legal pad, her immaculate handwriting swooping around in several cursive zeros.

"You want to know how much money you're going to bring in before the end of the month?"

"How much?"

"What's a nice car you've always wanted to own?"

"A Bentley. Bright blue."

"You'll have made enough money to buy seven of those. In cash." Margo politely folded the blank top sheet of the legal pad over the numbers with a satisfied smile. "Now we have to wait for the contracts to come in."

Despite being a house of five individuals, presumably all with busy schedules, Margo enforced a strict house dinner on Wednesday evenings at seven p.m. sharp. A personal chef was invited to the house in mid-morning to painstakingly prepare a meal from scratch, and tonight the dinner would be built around Vix's tastes, as a means of welcoming her into the fold. This was also the first time that Vix would meet the others. There was Iona and Margo, but also Lindsey (Twitch streamer, 500k followers), Greta (trained pastry chef, 150k followers), and Dharlyn (actress, 550k followers and no less than twenty IMDB acting credits.)

Margo sat at the head of the table, with Vix and

Iona on either side. Dharlyn seemed miffed when she entered the room, and Vix swore that her eyes almost ignited with rage when they locked with hers. But Dharlyn shrugged her shoulders and took her seat across from her.

"Hi, Vix. Lovely to meet you. Sorry; I've been on location in Savannah shooting a Netflix series. Eight episodes, ninety days, it's a whole mess." Dharlyn smiled but it was disingenuous. Then Vix realized she wasn't looking at her, she was looking at Margo, who didn't seem to notice. She was too preoccupied with her raspberry cheesecake Moscato. "It went well, by the way."

Margo seemed to suddenly notice Dharlyn's presence. "Oh, that's good to hear. The weather didn't get to you too much?"

Dharlyn rolled her eyes and looked at Vix directly. "I'm from Barbados. Humidity got nothing on me." A smile at Margo. "Ray says hi, by the way."

"Ray Payne?" Vix couldn't stifle her excitement. Heartthrob, heteronormative hunk, and half-way decent actor, Ray Payne? Was there any limit to the success that these women enjoyed? "He's working on a new show?"

Dharlyn pressed a finger to her lips, the corners of which turned up in a mischievous smile. "If the network doesn't shitcan it before it's released."

A sharp glare from Margo. "We're about to eat, Dharlyn."

In response, Dharlyn rolled her eyes and sighed.

Iona wordlessly passed the bottle of Moscato to her —a routine they had adopted for nights like this.

"What's on the menu tonight?" Iona asked, looking at Margo. "What did Vix pick?"

"She can tell us herself. What did you pick, Vix?" Margo asked.

Vix became painfully aware of all the eyes on her in the room, especially when Greta and Lindsey swooped in to take their seats. Somehow having this many eyes on her in person was scarier than the hundreds of thousands online.

And they took her silence as weakness. Greta, the pastry chef, piped up before she had a chance to reply. "You're from the Midwest, right? You're not going to make us eat a tater tot casserole, are you?"

"*I'm* from the Midwest. Have I ever made you eat a tater tot casserole?" Margo asked, while at the same time Lindsey rolled her eyes and said, "Do you even smell tater tots in that kitchen?"

Vix squirmed in her seat. "I actually asked for veggie burgers and a chickpea salad I used to make all the time."

"Oh! Chickpeas!" Iona seemed giddy. "*So* good for fat and protein, plus they're low-cal. I might actually be able to eat this dinner."

"You don't usually eat the dinners?"

Margo rolled her eyes. "Iona adheres to a very strict diet."

"But I'm always happy to sit and catch up," she pointedly added.

"You don't eat at dinner time?" Vix asked, still uncertain.

Iona's smile looked plastic. "I'm really big on IF."

"IF?"

"She means intermittent fasting." Dharlyn waved her hand dismissively.

Oh, of course she would be in a house with people who loved to fast. Once again Vix felt painfully aware of her too-chunky thighs. It felt like the fabric of her shorts were tightening around those sausages, raw meat squeezed into an expensive denim casing. Maybe she should have asked for lemon water and cucumbers with Tajín—then again, Iona would probably have something to say about the sodium content in any sort of seasoning. Flavor was not for skinny bitches. Certainly not for ones who got excited over raw chickpeas.

"You're not only going to eat the chickpea salad, right? You'll eat the burger, too?" Lindsey said. She had a bouncy, wavy blonde cut—a stark contrast to the other girls' shoulder-length hair. Her cat eyes were the envy of every e-girl, with sharp, thick lines and makeshift accentuated eyelashes. "I don't want Vix to think that we like, don't eat here."

"I eat," Iona protested, her voice thin. "But I have no idea what the chef is putting in the burger, so like..."

"Iona, you can't be serious. It's a veggie burger."

"Veggie burgers aren't all the same. They can be made like, hundreds of different ways. Just because they're "veggie" doesn't mean that they're actually full of veggies. Like, they can be full of grains or oats, and not a lot of veggies or beans or lentils at all—"

"—Iona, I think what Lindsey is trying to say is that it's not only rude to refuse to eat a meal that our chef graciously prepared, but one Vix specifically requested." Margo's voice was firm.

Iona's mouth clamped shut, too upset to say anything more. She glanced down at her phone. When the chef came around with their food, a couple of the girls cheered and eagerly dug in. Iona gingerly picked up her fork and started to eat the salad, picking it apart leaf by measly leaf. Margo took a sip from her glass of wine and shook her head. She set her glass down on the table and for some reason, the sound of the glass hitting the mahogany surface sounded a little too sharp, like the ringing of a bell.

"No, Iona. Eat the burger."

Iona looked up at her with pleading, quivering eyes, pitch-black pupils swimming in a sea of faint forest green. The other girls slowly turned to look in Iona's direction, almost synchronous, except each one was a half-second behind. Iona remained silent, fidgeting in her seat and picking at the scabby cuticles of her manicured fingers. When their gazes didn't break, she hung her head and folded her hands in her lap in defeat. Vix couldn't help but feel a little frightened at the intensity of the situation. It reminded her of her encounter with Josslyn. Women bled the most, so she supposed that's why they were the best at sniffing it out. Going in for the kill. Like sharks. And tonight, Lindsey was eager to be the toughest one at the table. Her hands clenched around her fork and knife, and with a heavy drum-beat, she pounded against the table. The thumps, combined with the musical clinking of the silver-ware, served as her rallying cry. Underneath it all, Vix could hear a small tinny sound in the back-ground, low and droning. At first, she didn't think much of it, till it grew in volume and vibrated under-neath her feet. Goosebumps sprung up on her arms and legs.

"Eat the burger! Eat the burger!"

Dharlyn joined, and so did Greta, and Margo, and Vix could only sit and stare at Iona as she increasingly became more terrified of the savory-smelling meal on her plate. She could've sworn Iona was blinking back tears. For a moment, she wanted to open her mouth and protest, say it was fine, but then she noticed Margo's sharp gaze, accompanied by her soft smile. Encouraging her to join in. And so Vix did. Their voices grew so loud and ravenous and gleeful that they shook the chandelier on the ceiling, and the lights—the lights, were they flickering in response? Iona finally lifted the burger to her mouth and tore off the tiniest of bites, clenching the morsels between her front teeth. Beef-like blood dripped onto the tablecloth, leaving little burgundy stains on its baby-pink surface. For a moment, Vix relaxed her chanting and slowed the pace of her drumming, but the girls only laughed and grew louder in volume, their voices as ferocious as Iona's growling stomach.

"EAT. . . THE. . . BURGER! EAT. . . THE. . . BURGER!"

And Iona shoved more and more of it into her gullet, swallowing as the tears pricked at the corners of her eyes. Vix could see the protruding lumps of food course their way down her butterfly-thin throat, making their way down like maggots wriggling below the surface of a rotting carcass. But as they went down, something came up—bile. Her body was rejecting the sustenance. Eyes watering, Iona gagged. She placed her clenched fist against her mouth to keep it in.

The girls did not relent. In fact, they jeered at her, taunting her to swallow. Iona stamped her feet against the ground like she was trying to crush cockroaches, rocking her head from side to side: frantic, possessed. Vix's body filled with panic. Choking, she was choking. But just when it seemed her body would exhaust its oxygen, Iona swallowed, the massive lump finally making its way to her stomach. Gasping for air, Iona finally freed her fist from its place. Saliva dripped from her mouth, glittering and stained raspberry-red from her smeared lip gloss.

"EAT THE BURGER! EAT THE BURGER! EAT THE BURGER!"

The tin-drone grew louder and louder, to the

point that it was almost deafening. The chandelier rattled around like chattering teeth in the cold. Vix could almost swear she saw the girls frothing at their mouths. Iona ate the burger more ferociously, her mannerisms resembling less of a human girl and more of a wolf. No biting, only tearing and shredding the food, eliminating it as fast as possible. The fear in Iona's face was gone, and something had overtaken her: primal, raw, and desperate for power.

"EAT THE BURGER! EAT THE BURGER! EAT THE BURGER!"

Within seconds, the burger was gone. The girls all cheered, some clinking glasses together. The tin-drone dissipated, and the vibration quieted beneath Vix's feet. The chandelier was still as if it had never moved in the first place. Iona fell back against her chair, panting and rubbing her sore stomach and throat. Her dilated pupils softened, and she looked like herself again. Breathless and red, she held up her glass for cheers, but the look on her face communicated that she would rather be dead than be at that table.

"Now no one can tell me I don't eat anymore," Iona said, holding up a finger reproachfully as she took a sip from her wine glass. "Clearly I eat faster than the rest of you bitches, so..."

Lindsey elbowed her playfully and the two laughed, but still, Iona's body remained tense. Unable to process the hostility at the dinner table any longer, Vix ate the rest of her meal. They sat there for two hours, topping off glass after glass, indulging in a homemade lemon sorbet, and chatting raucously about their various escapades. Despite the chaos from earlier, it was hard for Vix to not feel starstruck. Stories about pranking friends in lavish hotel rooms at conventions, group yoga sessions led as the sun crested over the Peruvian mountains, penthouse rooftop parties buzzing with the poshest and prettiest. Only a short time ago, Vix had been sweating it out in a roach-infested apartment and applying drugstore coverup to suspected bed bug-bites. Yes, these women were terrifying, but maybe that was less something for her to fear and more for her to admire. Better for a beautiful woman to be terrifying than terrorized, she decided.

After dinner cleared away, Margo invited Vix into her bedroom. Strips of twinkling LED lights framed the windows and doors: bright, blushing, glittering pink. They surrounded each of her biggest magazine covers. Interestingly—and somewhat disturbingly—a mounted deer head was placed in the center of these covers. Its stark bleach bones contrasted against the pastel walls. More LED lights, shaped like tear drops, were wrapped around its massive antlers. Nestled in the eyes of the skull, as well as woven through the strings of lights, were various flowers.

Margo noticed Vix taking everything in. She pointed to the hanging skull. "Family heirloom. Was my mother's before she passed on."

"A little. . . morbid, no?" Yet, just as she had in the office before, Vix couldn't help but feel drawn to it. She approached the antlers, resisting the desire to reach out and touch the soft little flowers.

"Many matriarchs in my family were." She tossed her hair over her shoulder. "They lived through famines, snowstorms, sicknesses. Many of them married seafaring men and had to carry on after ships capsized or exploded. They weren't strangers to death or morbidity by any means."

"These flowers. . . so pretty," Vix murmured. "I don't think I've ever seen anything like them."

"They're flowers native to Sweden." Margo stood alongside her, staring up at the decoration. "That purple one is the pasqueflower, meant to symbolize rebirth. And twinflowers, which are surprisingly scarce in some parts of the world."

"What are they meant to represent?"

Margo smiled and shrugged her shoulders. "I don't think they're meant to represent anything. Some great-grandmother or great-great-grandmother or another just wanted flowers from the homeland."

"I didn't realize your family's pedigree was so. . . intense. You're *all* Swedish?"

"Every last one of us. Swedish, or Swedish-American. Quite incestuous, I know."

"I wasn't. . ."

Vix trailed off, but Margo had already grown bored of the conversation. The model moseyed over to her vanity mirror, took a seat, and began to brush her hair. After a few luxurious strokes she paused, staring at Vix in her reflection.

"You look troubled for someone who was handed the world."

"I. . . Is Iona going to be okay?"

"Iona will be fine." Margo took a makeup wipe and scrubbed her face. "Is that what you're worried about? Eating a burger isn't going to kill her, Vix."

She thought about the foaming mouths of the girls, the way that the light had disappeared from Iona's pupils as she had succumbed to their tirade. "I suppose."

"Come here."

Margo reached into the drawer of the vanity and withdrew a small tube of something—cover-up or lipstick, she didn't know what. Margo patted her thigh and Vix came over. Margo patted her thigh again, and Vix slowly sat down on it, locking her arms around her neck. She stared at their reflections in the mirror. That familiar intoxicating feeling surfaced again in the pit of her stomach—desire, unkempt and untamed. Margo had been chaste since that day in her closet, hadn't so much as touched her, although Vix yearned to feel those skilled fingers between her thighs once more. Margo unscrewed the lid to the tube and swiped it against the inside of her wrist. It was sticky and red like lipstick, but also shimmery, some kind of gloss?

Margo tapped it on her cheek, and then rubbed some onto Vix's. *Oh*. Blush.

"When we first met, you told me you were the snake. But I think snakes have more bite than you do," Margo said. She reached a hand up to play with Vix's hair, curling it around and around her finger. "If you're going to play the part of the snake, you have to truly embrace it—hold nothing back. Do you think you could do that for me?"

Vix nodded.

"What about for yourself?"

Vix hesitated, but then she nodded again. Margo planted a kiss against her neck, warm and smooth like the blood coursing through her veins. Dizzy, Vix leaned into her touch. Margo smiled. She unlocked her phone and touched a button, and the LED lights darkened from pink to red. What followed after was nothing short of blissful and left Vix stumbling back to her bedroom on trembling legs.

Iona's bedroom was on the way to hers, and Vix saw from underneath the door, the faint remnants of blue light beneath. For some reason, the sight stopped her dead in her tracks. She checked her phone. It was 3:33 in the morning. She thought she heard soft music playing from behind the door, and she slowly approached. She raised a hand as if to knock, but then, underneath the din of the music, she heard something else—the sounds of someone retching. Guttural, deep, the sort of uncontrollable dry hacking that occurs when there's nothing left at the bottom of one's stomach. Stunned, she attempted to knock, but out of the shadows, someone grabbed her wrist.

Panicked, Vix whipped around to face the person, but she only saw Dharlyn, the outline of her face illuminated by the moonlight streaming in through the window. Dharlyn lowered Vix's hand and shook her head, her blonde boxer braids sashaying from side to side as she did so.

"Leave it."

"What do you mean, leave it?"

Dharlyn grabbed Vix's wrist more forcefully and pulled her away from the door. She looked at her with a tenacious intensity; her brown-eyed gaze stern and cold like steel.

"You cannot bother her when she's doing that."

"But she's bulimic. Shouldn't someone—"

"—She's not bulimic," Dharlyn said. "She has a doctor, besides that. You can't help her. Honestly, I don't think anyone can. She's committed to a life of this binging-purging shit, come hell or high water."

Vix stared at her, completely bewildered. How could she hear Iona throwing up in seclusion, in the middle of the night, and not think she was bulimic? Worse, how could she so blatantly remark that Iona was beyond saving? How could anyone be so callous towards someone who was suffering this much? But Dharlyn shook her head and flipped her hair over her shoulder.

"Look, you're new here. But if you talk to her

when she's like this, she's just going to become a raging bitch the next day. So, it's best to leave it." Dharlyn's eyes narrowed. She arched a curious brow and reached out to touch Vix. Her palm felt unusually warm to the touch. She pulled away her shirt collar, exposing a swollen love bite that Margo had left on her shoulder. "Ahh. So that's how it is."

"What do you—"

"—It's nothing. Don't worry about it." She zipped up her purse, then paused. "There're certain things you've got to be willing to give up here to succeed. I hope you're prepared for that."

"What?"

Dharlyn shook her head, as if too annoyed by Vix to provide further context. In turn, Vix tried to restrain the frustration rising in her voice.

"Where are you going?"

"So many questions." Dharlyn smiled, and for the first time that night, it seemed genuine. "I'm out. Ray's throwing some kind of cast party, and I'm already late. I'd invite you but. . ." She looked Vix up and down. "I think it's best you get some rest. You've had a long night."

Vix's cheeks burned with embarrassment. The cheek where Margo had stained her face with blush burned disproportionately hotter. Every part of her wanted nothing more than to tuck her tail between her legs and run from the room, but then she remembered what Margo had told her. *Be the snake.* She held her chin up high and squared her shoulders and crossed her arms. Appraised Dharlyn with that same coy smirk before proceeding to her room.

"Don't stay out too late."

The next morning, when Vix went to use the restroom, she saw Iona standing in front of the mirror, scrubbing at her mouth with a washcloth. She raised her head and saw Vix standing behind her in the reflection. Her lips formed a meager smile as her eyes, red-rimmed and tremendously swollen, stared at her. Vix smiled apologetically at her, although worry seized her stomach in a vice grip. Did Iona even go to bed last night?

"Hey. Everything okay?"

"I'm fine." Iona turned off the faucet and dragged the washcloth over her face again. "I think the veggie burger had gluten in it. It didn't agree with my stomach."

"Oh, I'm sorry to hear that." Vix struggled not to raise her eyebrows when she saw the corners of Iona's mouth were stained beet-red. "Iona, are you—"

"—I'm fine," Iona insisted.

She scrubbed at her face again, and it sounded bristly; like rubbing a stone against sandpaper. Vix could see the skin around her mouth was flaky and crispy like fish scales, so dehydrated it was on the verge of bleeding. Iona threw the washcloth in the hamper and darted from the room before Vix had a chance to intervene. Bewildered, Vix shut the door and locked it. She could see the toilet seat was stained red in parts as well: faded and blotchy like remnants of red wine on a white cashmere sweater. She made a mental note to tell Margo to send the cleaners here later—the whole place smelled ghastly, and even worse when the steam from her hot shower filled the room.

After a quick breakfast consisting of peanut butter oat balls and sugar-free iced coffee, Margo drove Vix to her first photoshoot of the day. She was whisked away by hair and makeup, who eagerly took to curling her hair and applying stark pink eyeshadow. She had no idea what she was supposed to be modeling until the stylist arrived with a variety of pieces to choose from. The look could be described as Japanese schoolgirl mixed with old school grunge. Pleated plaid skirts with kawaii skulls emblazoned across the front and black dresses lined with red lace. A little bit e-girl, a little bit not, but everything hot. Vix admired herself in front of the mirror countless times as the morning proceeded. Margo preened and prodded and poked, cleaning up all the "little mistakes." A stray eyebrow hair, a clump of mascara on her lash, a cheek blemish that hadn't been covered. Although some of the makeup artists were bristly about their job being done for them, ultimately, Margo held the power within the room, and they let her have her way.

After fixing her up, Margo snapped her fingers,

and wordlessly, the various assistants exited, leaving them alone in the dressing room. Vix sat in front of the vanity, her eyelids heavy from the thick lashes they had applied. Margo beamed with pride, and with a happy sigh, locked her arms around Vix's neck.

"It never gets old," she commented, "watching the newbies do their first fashion shoot. How do you feel?"

"Nervous," Vix said with a laugh. "But also excited."

"Excited is good. So is nervous. You want me to give you a tip before you go out there?"

"Any tips that you could offer would be amazing, Margo." She needed all the help that she could get, and who better to ask than a world famous Insta-model?

"When they go for the side profile, you're going to want to try something. It's an age-old trick. Have you heard of mewing?"

"Mewing?" Vix giggled. "Like a kitten?"

"It's a technique, actually," Margo said. "It helps to reshape your jawline. Here. Close your mouth."

Vix did as she was told.

"Now. Your tongue. Pretend you have peanut butter on the roof of your mouth, and press your tongue up there."

Vix dropped her jaw and Margo *tut-tutted* gently. "No. Keep your mouth shut. Press your tongue up against the roof of your mouth, behind your teeth."

Vix obeyed. She turned her head to the side and was almost shocked to see the difference. A smooth, clean and defined jawline, connecting her face to her throat with nary a bump. She relaxed her tongue, and when she did so, it was like rolls of fat melted into their place. Margo smiled.

"Yeah, I thought you'd like the tip." She combed her fingers through Vix's hair once more and fluffed it. "Are you ready?"

Vix nodded. And then, like a show pony at a small-town rodeo, Vix was trotted out in front of a green screen and dozens of intense, hot lights. She stood, bleary eyed and nervous in front of the staff. Dozens of people huddled in front of her, their eyes wide and full of reverence, like she was a prophet preaching to her disciples. But only one set of eyes mattered to her in that crowd: Margo's.

The photographer introduced himself. Gregg or Scott or maybe it was Taylor. She didn't remember since she was too distracted by the heat of the lights. It felt like her makeup was peeling off her skin. But somehow, when he raised his camera, her nervousness washed away. She locked eyes with Margo in the darkness.

Be the snake.

Vix struck a pose and didn't even blink in the white-hot flash of light that soon followed. Another, and another, and then—"Okay! Next outfit, please!" —a rush back to wardrobe and a touch-up by hair and makeup. Back out, back in, and each time she appeared in front of the camera she was all the more radiant, capturing the attention of everyone there. When the photoshoot wrapped, they clapped for her. Several commented on her professionalism, on her innate talent, on all the things she had ever wanted to hear. Glowing with pride, she climbed into the car with Margo that night, and thanked her for every single success she had brought her thus far.

"I hope you're ready, honey," Margo murmured, tucking a strand of hair behind her ear. "Because you're about to be a star."

PART TWO

Within months, Vix became the top new model. She appeared on Lindsey's gaming channel, served as a sous chef for some of Greta's baking videos, and tried her hand at some of Iona's TikTok fitness challenges. Her Instagram ballooned to numbers comparable to that of Dharlyn's. Soon her face was everywhere. Billboards, magazines, Facebook ads. Margo created a YouTube account for her, and twice a week, she uploaded videos that involved her unboxing beauty products or discussing the latest fashion trends. When not at the house, she was being shuffled to photoshoots and industry parties. It was exhausting but exhilarating, and the best part was she could even afford to send home money to her mother and grandmother in Kansas, but despite this, they scarcely spoke. Her mother was never much of a texter to begin with, but once she snapped a photo of a magazine cover and sent it to her with the caption, "Your pretty auburn hair," and a broken heart emoji. Less than five words, and yet it was a total assault on Vix's solitude. Immediately, she flew into a fiery rage, but Margo had prevented the wildfire from spreading.

"She'll stop complaining eventually. Keep sending the checks," Margo assured her. "You're not doing this for her approval. You're doing this for yourself. She'll learn to be grateful—and if she's not, I trust you'll make the right decision."

Although Margo reigned supreme in the household, Vix was happy to rule by her side. Prideful, even, when Margo took her to those lavish parties and introduced her to bigwigs who would stare at her cleavage a bit too long. And Margo would talk about her in grandiose fashion, like she was so surprised and blown away by all of Vix's success, despite the fact she had fabricated it for her. Margo considered her important, and that made Vix important to other people. Being a Bleach Babe wasn't the only thing she loved; it was being loved by Margo.

But after the fourth month at the mansion, it felt like some of the spark from their relationship had fizzled. The jobs were still coming in, and Vix would never want for anything ever again, but at times, she saw a troubled expression cross Margo's face. When she asked her about it, Margo was polite yet dismissive, reassuring her everything was fine and then redirecting her to the next task at hand. It was in those moments that Vix could feel her exterior molting; that she felt so pathetically lonely when Margo declined to share bits and pieces of her life with her, it almost drove her to tears. The fifth time it happened, she actually did break down, but only after stumbling up the stairs and into Lindsey's room. She was almost nonsensical in her grief, as she bawled to Lindsey about Margo's iciness, the way she could feel her pulling away.

"Girl, you worry too much," she said. "This is the time when a lot of girls tend to leave the house."

"What?"

"Most of the Bleach Babes don't live here. You know that. They usually live here for a few months to get up off the ground, and then they go out into the world and do their own thing. She probably doesn't want to get too attached in case you want to leave. Well, and she might not be feeling so great since Dharlyn is leaving—"

Vix was shocked. "—Dharlyn is *leaving*?"

"She's moving in with Ray, Vix. I'm surprised you didn't know that. She's barely around."

Vix had learned from Margo that Dharlyn had been at the house the longest—had lived there a whole four years, whereas Lindsey, Iona, and Greta had only been there for a year or two at most. Dharlyn met, and started dating, Ray while spending more and more time preparing for their show's release. Margo's attitude made sense now:

not only had she lost Leilani in the past year, she was also losing Dharlyn, and it was inevitable Vix would leave too.

"Hey." Lindsey reached forward and squeezed Vix's hand. "I know you care a lot about her. I'm not quite sure what's, like, going on between the two of you, but if you want to show your loyalty to her, y'know, that could go a long way. She's a fan of big gestures like that."

"What kind of big gestures?" Margo was not the stand-outside-with-a-boom-box kind of girl.

Lindsey exhaled slowly, her blue eyes wide and unblinking. She shook her head and twiddled her thumbs.

"I would ask Iona, actually." Lindsey scratched her head. "Maybe like. . . six months after Iona had moved in here, something happened between the two of them. I can't recall exactly. Maybe it was that she still had a bank account? Or she had a call with an agent? It violated the rules, for sure. And Iona had to do something to make it up or risk getting cold-shouldered out of the house. But I don't know what it was."

Since the morning that Vix had caught her throwing up in the toilet, she and Iona were on thin, but friendly terms. They collabed and spoke to one another, but Vix had been unable to develop any kind of closeness with her like she had with Lindsey and Greta. Still, it was worth a try. So after finishing her conversation with Lindsey, Vix descended the stairs and moved into the sun room, where Iona was engaging in a sun salutation. In the light of the ripe-orange morning sun, she could see the little knobs along Iona's spine sticking out. She winced. Iona exhaled and brought her arms down.

"What do you need, Vix?"

"I'm trying to do something for Margo," Vix said. She weaved through the mass of potted plants spread across the floor. If not for the mirror and exercise equipment, the place would look like the landscaping section at the Home Depot. "I was hoping I could ask you about it."

"Do what for Margo? Her birthday isn't for another couple of months."

"No, it's. . ." Vix quietly launched into her stammery explanation, and watched as Iona's eyes grew darker and darker like an abyss. But still, Iona didn't move, didn't so much as shake her head. Breathlessly, as she finished, Vix asked, "Would you be willing to help me?"

"You. . ." Iona trailed off, her voice equally low and nervous. "I don't think you need to do that for her. You're already, like, so successful, Vix. I'm sure she's proud of you as is."

"I need to do this," Vix insisted.

"But it's dangerous!" Iona blurted, and she clapped her hand over her mouth.

"But you did it, didn't you?" Maybe Leilani had too. Maybe that's why she had gone missing. Whatever it was, it was a huge risk to undergo, but it would be worth it if it meant making Margo happy. "Please, Iona. I have to make her see that I can, and want, to stay with the Bleach Babes. I don't want her to pull away from me."

Iona paused and took a deep breath, her eyes haunted. "Okay. But you need to not judge me when I tell you what you have to do. Because it's really out there. But it's like, the best way to show Margo your commitment." Another pause. "You're sure about this, right?"

Vix nodded vigorously. Iona leaned in, nearly pressing her lips against Vix's ear, and whispered the secret to her.

* * *

The weight of what Iona told Vix made her nauseous, but she tried to remain calm. Iona packed up her yoga mat and retreated into her room to edit more videos for her channel. After taking a few deep breaths, Vix stumbled into the kitchen for coffee, and she crossed paths with Dharlyn. She almost did a double take. Every time she had seen Dharlyn, her hair had either been dyed blonde, or had blonde extensions. Today, Dharlyn was wearing her hair in cornrows, but they weren't blonde—they were ombre green and sky blue. They looked so vibrant in the light of their too-pink kitchen.

"Hey," Dharlyn said, glancing Vix up and down.

"Damn. I know you're pale, but like, you're virtually translucent. Are you hungover or something?"

"Oh, no. . ."

Dharlyn was simultaneously unconvinced and concerned. "You should probably have something to eat and take it easy then."

"I think I have to fast this morning." Vix groaned and rubbed a hand over her eyes. She could never remember the schedule the dietician had put her on. She opened her app to clarify—yep, today was another fasting day. "I can only have, at most, coffee. And technically that's cheating."

"Margo put you on a diet?"

"The dietician put me on a diet." Vix reached into the fridge and poured herself a cup of iced coffee. All the sounds in the room sounded amplified: the pouring of liquid into her mug, the soft scraping of Dharlyn's spoon as she took a bite out of her grapefruit. She shook her head, but she couldn't stop the ringing.

"Yeah, she tried to put me on that diet too. She's a quack." Dharlyn rolled her eyes and took a bite of her grapefruit. She stabbed the spoon back into the fruit with an odd forcefulness. "You better be careful with what she says. You don't want to fuck up your metabolism like I did."

Vix swallowed. "Hey, uh. . . I heard from Lindsey that you were leaving. Is it true?"

"Yeah. Why?"

Vix took a sip of her coffee and wiped the back of

her mouth with her hand. "I was surprised. You've been here for a long time. It's going to be hard without you."

Dharlyn squinted. "Is it?"

"W-well, yeah. I think. . . I think Margo's a little upset about it."

"Margo's upset?" Dharlyn smiled and propped her chin up on her hand.

"I think so. She's been short with me lately."

"Margo is short with everyone. It's kind of how she is."

Vix resisted the burning urge to rush to her mentor's defense by swallowing another sip of coffee. Dharlyn sighed, breaking her intense stare. She took another bite of her food and then laid down her spoon.

"Margo is upset because Margo wants control, and once you leave the house and set up your own bank accounts again, she can't control you anymore."

"But you're still a part of the Bleach Babes, aren't you?"

"Of course. I'm fine with every other girl here. But Margo takes this shit personally. I wouldn't be surprised if I stop getting invited to all our house parties."

"Well. . . I mean. . ."

Vix wanted to ask her why she was leaving, but she knew the answer was obvious. Because of Ray, her new hotshot boyfriend. But what had happened? What had caused Dharlyn to be so upset that she took out her blonde extensions? To divorce herself from the group in such a visibly dramatic way?

"Stop looking at my hair like you think it means something," Dharlyn told her. She rolled her eyes. "That's part of the problem. Grown ass adults in this house, and no one is allowed to have any individuality. Someone changes the color of their hair, and you treat them like a leper."

"I'm not treating you like a leper, I'm—"

"—You are. You're looking at me like I have two heads."

"That's not true," Vix shot back, and she was surprised by her viper-tongue. "And by the way, if we don't have individuality, why do we have separate careers? Like, why is Lindsey allowed to be a gamer and Greta is a baker and—"

"—Because that's how the collective makes money. Through diversifying what kind of content we put out there and what kind of people she accepts into it. It's a little bit of something for everyone. But this house? What she does? It's how she stays in control. And I'm sick of it. I'm sick of her acting like she knows everything and dictating what I can or can't wear, eat, or work on. You know how many trips I've had to turn down because she takes those mandatory dinners so strictly? You know how rough that's been with Ray?" Dharlyn shook her head ferociously. "Vix, look. You haven't been in this too long, so you can still walk away. There's a chance. It won't be as hard for you as it was for me, or Leilani."

Vix faltered at the mention of the missing girl. The beautiful one whose smile haunted her every time she walked into Margo's office. The one who she replaced. The one who she thought Margo still longed for but would never say outright.

"Leilani left? Successfully?"

"Successfully? What the hell do you mean by. . ." Dharlyn sighed when she realized what Vix was implying. "I'm *assuming*, Vix. She left a note. But she had to abandon her entire life so she could be free from Margo. That's what you're signing up for."

"But why would I want to walk away? It's not like Margo has done anything wrong. She has the rules in place for a reason, and it's turning into success. No one would dare give me a sponsorship or any kind of modeling gig until I joined the Bleach Babes. And now that I'm here, it's like people can't get enough of me."

Dharlyn sighed again. She pinched the bridge of her nose, a clear sign that she was frustrated with the conversation, but Vix pressed on.

"We do good work here. Margo does *good* for us."

Dharlyn laughed. "Do you really think what we're doing is good?"

Vix faltered. Something about the glint in Dharlyn's eyes told her there was something else lying underneath the surface of that response, possibly something more that she knew about Leilani. But as soon as she noticed, Dharlyn blinked it away.

"I get this is exciting for you. And I get that you wouldn't have gotten here without her. I'm not saying I would've either. But this place? This level of control on a day-to-day basis? It's going to get to you. And without Ray, I wouldn't have felt like I could leave."

"Why?" Vix sputtered into laughter. The melodrama was almost too much for her to handle. "You think Margo would hunt you down otherwise?"

Dharlyn shrugged her shoulders. Pressed her lips firmly together. "It's no use talking to you about any of this, honestly. I can tell you're still moony for Margo, so nothing I say is going to register with you."

"It would if you actually made any sense."

"Oh yeah, Vix." Her eyes sharpened with anger. "Way to tell the Black woman she's crazy."

Vix felt a pang. "No! N-no, Dharlyn, I didn't mean it—"

"—And this is the reason why this place isn't as good as you think it is." She sighed, stood up, and placed her bowl in the sink. She picked up the grapefruit rind and tossed it into the compost container by the faucet. She gripped the edges of the counter, her head hanging low. Her voice was soft and gentle. "It's not your fault you can't see it now. But you will one day. And I hope that's not going to be too late."

She shuffled past Vix, her expression now seeming sad. She gently patted Vix's shoulder and moved out of the kitchen.

That was the last time she saw Dharlyn. Later that afternoon, a moving company came to take the furniture from her bedroom and five suitcases worth of clothes. She didn't say goodbye in person but did so online: a picture of her kissing Ray's cheek and flashing off an engagement ring in their new condo. Given that the two had only been dating a few months, the Bleach Babes were in shock over this, but none more so than Margo. Margo's eyes burned bright red, but she didn't cry. She just sat in her office chair and looked out the window, barely responding to the girls when they tried to comfort her. Vix shuffled back into Margo's office a few hours later to check on her once more and found her in the same exact position.

"Something about the sky today seems so hopeful, don't you think?" Margo asked.

Vix nodded, although she didn't know what she meant. "You should eat. It's time for dinner."

"Later." Margo sighed. Finally, it came, in a quiet whisper: "I don't understand why she was so unhappy here."

Vix shrugged.

"She was happy once."

"I don't think it's anything you can control, Margo."

Uh oh. That wasn't good to say. Margo snapped

her head up and looked at Vix intensely. "Are you saying I'm controlling?"

"Well, no."

"No, but?"

Vix sighed. "I spoke to Dharlyn. Before she left."

"And?" Margo arched her brow.

Suddenly Vix's mouth felt so dry, like there were cotton balls shoved down her throat. "And she just mentioned she didn't want to live in the house anymore because of all the rules. Like, she thought it was controlling."

"Oh." Margo relaxed. "I see. That's nothing new, then. Nothing she hasn't said before."

"So you've been having those talks with her?"

"I do, in fact, talk to people other than you, Vix."

"That's not what I meant, I. . ." Vix trailed off. She felt like Margo's words, thick with iciness, were on the verge of stabbing her, lacerating her whole body, and unveiling her vulnerable heart beneath. "Margo, did I do something wrong?"

"What do you mean?"

"It's just that lately you've seemed so distant. I guess Dharlyn leaving like, is affecting you, but—"

"—but what?"

"I want to make sure we're still okay."

Margo nodded slowly. "We are."

Vix squirmed, unconvinced. She felt like caterpillars were crawling inside of her body; she was so jittery. "Then why doesn't it feel like it?"

"I don't know, Vix." Margo blinked, her long

lashes touching the tops of her cheeks. "Would it have anything to do with what I overheard in the kitchen this morning?"

"What?"

"I heard you arguing with Dharlyn and she stormed out."

"How did you—"

"—We have a security camera sitting on the top of the fridge. I didn't listen at first—I was busy fixing up some other photos at the moment. But I heard her laugh in that bitchy little way of hers, and that's when I knew things were flying south."

"How much did you. . . Margo, no, it was. . ." Vix placed her hands over her heart. "I didn't do anything. She was talking shit about you! About the Bleach Babes!"

"And what did she say?"

"That she. . . I don't know, something about suppressing individuality, and like. . . she doesn't think it's a good idea anymore."

"She doesn't think that it's good?" Margo laughed haughtily, as if the idea was too ludicrous for her to wrap her head around. "You know, it's quite funny, really. She rose to fame using the same tactics I, and other influencers, have used, but now, she wants to pretend they're bad? Before the Instafluencers, you know what we saw in the world of fashion? Wispy little WASPs without a brain in their heads or an original thought. Just, 'Yes, sir, no, sir.' *They* didn't create anything. Men created it for them, and they were the mannequins. In this age, *we* get to take the power. We can dress as we like, do our makeup as we like, cut and dye our hair fifty different ways to Sunday, and no one can say a goddamn thing about it. We are gods. Is everything we do ethical? No, but nothing is truly ethical. At least girls are no longer being pressured to starve themselves."

Vix nodded slowly. What Margo said made a lot of sense, and in many ways, she was right. In actuality, a lot of men were the ones making the decision in the fashion world, not women. Models were living dolls meant to be dressed up and trotted out like dogs at the Westminster show; they were viewed as playthings and not people. Even in the pageant world, where girls had to answer questions regarding public policy and grand moral questions, it was still manufactured. They were forced to present an idea of themselves that they thought *others* would want to see, not who they truly were. But even though Vix agreed with Margo that things were better now, that entire response didn't sit quite right.

"But the culture still exists, doesn't it? I mean, Iona. . ."

"What about Iona?"

Vix didn't understand Margo's confusion. The occasional past-midnight purging sessions. Her bony body. Her bizarre fixation on counting calories and eating organic and avoiding gluten like it was cyanide.

"Her... bulimia? Her orthorexia?"

"What the fuck is orthorexia?"

"I-it's when you hyperfixate on eating healthy foods and—I mean, she has an eating disorder."

Margo's eyes flashed. Betrayed, betrayed, betrayed. She spoke in a wounded tone of voice, every other syllable almost too low for her to hear. "And you're blaming that on me, Vixen? That's so fucked up."

Panic swelled every cell in her body. "I wasn't blaming you; I'm saying there's a culture that—"

"—Oh my God. You are just like Dharlyn." Margo was seething, her shoulders bristling, but she spoke in a far-off, distant tone. "I told you to become the snake and here you are, a doe-eyed little Bambi acting like I chased her through the woods and shot her mother in the back of the fucking head. Did I do that, Vix? Did I personally *hurt* you?"

"No, *never!*" Vix felt as if all the air had been sucked from her body and she found it difficult to stand. "M-Margo, I'd never accuse you of doing something so awful. I was only bringing up what Dharlyn had said, I—"

"—Do you still have faith in me, Vix?" Margo asked sternly.

"Faith in—"

"—That I can take care of you? Show you everything this life has to offer?"

The answer left her lips instantaneously: "Yes." She shook her head. "Margo, I'd do anything to prove that to you. You know that." she swallowed. "And actually, I. . . I spoke to Iona today. This morning. Because I knew she had done something to prove her loyalty to you, and I wanted to do it."

For the first time since they had met, Margo seemed stunned. "You're *sure* you want to do that?"

"I'm positive."

Something painful surfaced in Margo's eyes for a moment. The red veins of her cornea glistened as if strained, like she had been staring at her computer screen for too long. She probably had been. But judging by the lump she was swallowing, it wasn't exhaustion.

Sadness.

"It worked for Iona, but. . . Leilani. . ." Margo shook her head. "Leilani didn't listen. She didn't listen to me, and she ended up. . . she ended up. . ."

"I don't care. I don't care what happened to her, I'm telling you I'm not going to make the same mistake." Vix approached her and with trembling hands, took Margo's in hers. "Whatever you want me to do, I'll do it. No ask too big or too small."

Margo's eyes locked on hers, and it was electrifying. Vix could feel her knees quake beneath her, and she wanted to lean in so desperately and kiss those pink plush lips, but she resisted the urge. Margo slowly nodded. She squeezed Vix's hands and did not let them go.

"Alright then."

* * *

The theater room was located adjacent to the living room, on the opposite end of the rising sun. Massive blackout curtains were almost always drawn shut, so as to protect the integrity of the massive screen that hung on the wall. Movie theater seating, upholstered with the plumpest of cushions, lined up in three neat rows of five. When Margo led Vix into the room, she was at first confused as to why they were there, but she knew better than to ask questions. Margo entered the projector room and went over to what Vix had always assumed to be a closet door. Margo opened it and stepped inside. It was crammed with cleaning supplies, a popcorn machine, and other various household items. After removing a broom and a vacuum, a soft *click* reverberated through the air. Margo stuck her head out of the closet.

"Okay. Come on."

Vix stepped into the closet beside her, and in the darkness, she could see what had made the click: a door, and on the other side, a long concrete staircase leading down into an inky-black abyss. Margo reached inside, flicked on a switch, and a fluorescent light sputtered to life. It barely illuminated the pathway ahead. Instinctively, Vix reached for Margo's hand, but Margo moved forward, out of reach, and down the stairs. Vix followed. There was no railing, so every step she took was careful.

"I didn't realize that there were basements in California."

She could see Margo looking over her shoulder. "Some houses do have them, although it's quite rare. It's nice to have the utilities in the basement, rather than taking up space in other parts of the house. Of course, we've repurposed this room for other means..."

They reached the bottom of the stairs, and Margo flicked on another light. A series of LEDs, rimming the edges of the room, turned red upon ignition. At the back, a circuit box and a water heater, slowly rumbling. There were various paintings draped in cloth; old, framed photographs; and discarded pieces of vlogging equipment scattered on shelves and in boxes throughout the room. On the floor was a red stain akin to rust, but judging from the coppery smell in the air, it was anything but. Vix's stomach somersaulted, and she considered fleeing up the stairs, but she would not succumb to her dread. She wasn't doing this for herself; this was for Margo.

And she would do anything for Margo.

"I understand this sounds a little crazy, right?" Margo asked, her voice shifting upwards in pitch. "When I was a teenager, I did this with my mother. It was a tradition that had been passed down through generations on her side of the family."

"Was your mother a. . ."

"Was she what?"

"Well, it seems. . . vaguely. . . pagan in nature." Much like the deer skulls that adorned the office and Margo's bedroom.

"I don't know whether she was a witch or not if that's what you're asking. All I know is what she did for me helped my success, Iona's success, and now finally, yours. And once it's done, we'll be bonded in sisterhood for life." Margo gently reached out and touched her shoulder, almost affectionately. "You do know I can't be in the room with you when it happens, right?"

Vix nodded. "I understand."

"And no matter how much you scream, I can't let you out? You only get one shot at this."

"I understand, Margo." Vix took her hand and kissed it.

For a moment, she thought Margo flinched, but whatever discomfort she saw was gone in a split second and replaced with that super-sweet smile. Margo tucked back a strand of her hair and pressed her forehead against Vix's.

"Stand right here, in the center of the room."

Vix obeyed. Margo went over to a shelf where a small mahogany box sat. The edges had various carvings and it appeared quite old, almost like a repurposed music box. She reached into it and withdrew a piece of chalk. Margo turned back to her.

"Stay perfectly still."

Vix obeyed. She watched as Margo crouched down to the stained floor and began to sketch the outline of a circle, then fill in the outline with intricate lines, triangles, and designs. A crude deer skull, various wounded eyes, and delicate feminine hands with long, pointed nails. As the minutes passed by, an intricate tapestry formed at Vix's feet. An innermost circle was drawn at the tips of Vix's toes.

"As long as you stay in this circle, you'll be protected." Margo placed the chalk back inside the box, and then withdrew a pair of matches. But these matches looked different. They were long and spindly like incense sticks and pink like a fresh peony on a spring day. With precision, Margo struck the match against the box and held it pinched between her two fingers.

"Are you ready?" Margo asked.

Vix nodded. "I'm ready."

Margo began to speak in a tongue Vix didn't recognize—at first it sounded vaguely Latin, but Margo thought she recognized some phrases here and there in Swedish, Margo's native tongue. She watched as Margo crouched down and used the match to ignite the tapestry. The tiny flames surrounded her feet, and at first, she wanted to jump out of their reach, but Margo's stern voice discouraged her.

"Do *not* leave the circle, Vixen. If you leave the circle I cannot protect you." Her voice dropped to a low murmur. "I don't want you to end up like Leilani."

Vix glanced at the red stain beneath her feet and with a sickening realization, understood this was all that remained of the girl she had replaced. But she would not be like Leilani. She was good; she was obedient; she was committed. Vix squeezed her eyes shut. She could feel the heat of the flames intensifying as they drew closer and larger, but somehow, they didn't scorch her. Margo continued to chant, her voice undulating now in bizarre ways that didn't sound humanly possible, making her all the more powerful.

When she finished, her voice fell away in a hiss, getting lost in the crackling of the fires below. She held up a small vial to Vix's nose, presumably from the same box as the matches and chalk. It reeked of sulfur and sand. Margo lifted her hands upwards and inhaled through her nostrils, and Vix copied her. She felt various *pops* inside her head, as if each one of her synapses was suddenly firing inside her brain.

"When He speaks to you, tell Him earnestly what you want. And once you give Him your wish, and agree to His demands, we will be bonded for eternity. Do not leave the circle, and I will see you on the other side."

Vix nodded, not bothering to open her eyes. She heard Margo's footsteps recede and the gentle flick of the light switch before she walked up the stairs and shut the door. Vix swallowed. She knew without opening her eyes that she was suspended in darkness. She also knew, instinctively, that although Margo had left, she was not alone. She pressed her feet closer together inside the circle and squared her shoulders, trying to keep herself firmly planted within. The house rumbled as the silence wore on, vibrating beneath her feet.

Vix heard something call out to her in the darkness, a soft, familiar voice over the din of the crackling flames. Calling her name. And finally, Vix felt brave enough to open her eyes. Flanking her on either side of the room was the basement, but directly ahead, its edges like a watercolor painting bleeding into her reality, was her kitchen back home. And in it, her mother and grandmother. Her mother was washing dishes in the sink, and her grandmother was paging through her various fashion magazines. Tears pricked at the corners of Vix's eyes, and she choked back a sob. She hadn't seen her family for so long. But these people weren't real, were they?

Her mother, with her auburn hair cut short and coiffed, looked over her shoulder. "There you are. Are you going to help me wash these dishes?"

Vix's knees twitched, as if to move her out of the circle. But she gritted her teeth and stayed. She stared at her mother-not-mother, who looked back at her with hollow eyes. Even though this apparition was a stranger, she was terrifyingly familiar. Her "mother" shook her head and turned her attention back to the dishes.

Gran looked at her daughter. "She's here to visit, Patty. Guests don't need to do dishes."

"She's a guest?"

"She doesn't live here anymore."

"And who's fault is that?" Patty shut off the faucet with a forceful squeak, and for a moment, Vix thought she heard her own scream swimming within the noise. She patted her hands dry with a tattered dish towel and turned to face her daughter. "Look at her. Look at what she did to her hair. It's *ruined.*"

"Hair is hair," Gran insisted with a dismissive wave. "And kids dye their hair. Regardless of whether or not it's damaged forever, it's her decision to make."

"Is it?" Patty turned her attention to Vix.

She could see the veins on her mother's forehead bulging, a telltale sign she was on the verge of a migraine—and a screaming meltdown. Patty blinked repeatedly, her passive aggressive way of asking, *Are you going to say anything?* But Vix didn't move. She stayed in place and watched as her mother skirted over to the pantry. She opened the cabinet door, revealing the spice rack that rested behind it. Gran shook her head over and over again but said nothing. Patty reached inside the pantry and grabbed a flask. She took a sip and pointed at her daughter with a pruny finger.

"You're not making decisions for yourself anymore. I barely recognize you."

Now Vix finally spoke, "I *am* making decisions for myself. You're just mad that I'm not making the decisions you want me to make."

"I'm mad my daughter is whoring herself out on the Internet."

Gran slapped her magazine down on the table. "That's enough, Patricia! You're starting to sound like Randy. And if you don't like it, don't cash the checks she sends." Gran looked at her with a face of disapproval. "You have to forgive her, Vixen. It's been hard for her to let go."

"It's been hard for me too. But I need you to know I don't regret a single decision I've made." Vix swallowed, gazing at her mother ferociously. "This is empowering for me, and that's what you can't stand. You can't stand that you can't control me anymore."

"You little *bitch*—" Patty roared, stomping towards her at a frightening speed.

Vix squeezed her eyes shut. She could feel her mother's hot breath on her face, could smell the alcohol in it, but as soon as she did, it was gone. And with it, any sort of affection she had for her and her home. Gone was her fear, along with her compassion and sense of connection with her family. It was as if her brain had been instantaneously rewired. She heard a voice, speaking to her in the darkness, low and rumbling, like a thunderstorm in the night.

"You. . . know who. . . is next. . . ?" It asked her, neither man nor spirit, something above her. The voice was devoid of emotion, but its words were almost taunting. Vix knew who would follow.

She opened her eyes again and saw, for the first time in years, her father. Potbellied and grizzled, yet his face was so gaunt it was almost skeletal. He sat in a chair where her family kitchen had once stood. Behind him, she could see the peeling edges of olive-green wallpaper, and beneath it, blackened spots. He, like the room he was in, was a fierce fungal infection. And she would be all too glad to purge her feelings for him, good and bad.

Predictably, he was holding a cheap bottle of beer—a Coors or a Samuel Adams, she couldn't tell —and as he locked eyes with her, he took a sip, and rocked back in his chair.

"Look at you, huh." He chuckled and shook his head. His brows were so heavy and thick that they nearly eclipsed his sunken-in eyes. "When you bleached your hair, did you bleach your brain cells too?"

Vix remained silent. Her dad rolled his eyes.

"I see a few of your pictures here and there. Your Aunt Heather told me about them. I'm surprised they let girls like you wear those kinds of clothes, to be honest." He wrinkled his nose, as if disgusted. "Don't take this the wrong way, but I liked the real rail-thin girls they used to have, back in the day. Heroin chic. You know what that means? Heroin chic. That's what they were called." A sip. "Don't make much sense to have a model with a few rolls, you know what I mean? Still. Good for you." A laugh, cold like a cough. "I was real worried about you, when you were a kid. You used to eat so much I thought you'd eat us out of house and home. Glad to see you've curbed that, but I bet if you lost a little more, you'd be even bigger."

"I will decide what I want to do with my own body," Vix protested, her voice calm. "And I don't care to hear your opinions any longer."

"Too bad." He shrugged his shoulders. "I paid my child support. Far as I'm concerned, I damn well have the right to tell you what I think every day for the rest of my life. Does that hurt your little feelings?"

"It used to."

A twinkle in his dark, beady little eyes. "Used to? Are you sure about that?"

"Why do you want to hurt me?"

He shrugged. "When you were in your mother's belly, the doctors kept telling me I would have a boy. A boy. I'd wanted a boy from the minute your mother told me that she was pregnant. But when we got to that first ultrasound and I found out what you really were, well. . . that was the single worst moment of my life." He took another sip of his beer, and looked past her, almost off in the distance. "I thought about it, y'know. Ways to get rid of you. Part of me wondered what would happen if I shoved Patty down the stairs. Thought about how I could make it look like an accident. I entertained those thoughts for so many months, and those thoughts? They got me through those dark, dark times.

"I mean, you have to imagine what it was like for me. You sign your life away to someone, and she gives you a *girl*? The first girl born in your family in generations?" He shook his head, the coldness returning to his expression. He rocked back and forth, and the chair creaked in protest. "You had my Daddy looking at me like something was wrong with me. And I couldn't shake that. Women are good for a few things, but men carry on legacies. Men are champions. What are you the champion of? Looking like plastic? You think that's an accomplishment?"

Vix sighed. She didn't even feel sad anymore. All she felt was annoyance. Who was this drunken peasant, and why did he feel entitled to speak to her that way? And why had she, for so many years, let him hold such power over her?

The voice spoke again. "You can. . . do it. . . if you. . . want. . ."

Vix realized that her hand was clasped around something. She opened her eyes and looked down at her left hand to see what it was. The curved hilt of a knife. It seemed to glow amber in the firelight. And suddenly, she was standing almost directly over her father. At first, she panicked, thinking that she had left the circle, but in fact, the circle had moved her.

The little flames still danced at her feet. Her father's eyes glinted at her in the dim light.

"You don't have the balls."

Vix sighed. So, so annoying. Like a fly whizzing around inside her brain. "Fuck it."

And she plunged the knife into his heart, splitting his booze-stained plaid shirt in half, and staining it bright red. Crimson blood spurted out like a geyser, coating the front of Vix's shirt and pink pleated skirt. His eyes, once receded, bulged out of his head, and his mouth opened in a breathless, surprised scream. The beer bottle fell on the ground and stained the hay-colored carpet brown. He stared up at her, as if begging for mercy, and Vix removed the knife.

Then she plunged it back in.

Again and again.

At first his screams were loud, but soon the sounds coming from his mouth were nothing but the sounds of fire: crackling, swirling, roaring. It was interesting, really, how his body seemed to deflate the more blood leaked from the hole in his chest—like the sad Dollar Store piñata he had gotten her for her fifth birthday party. When she finished, he stared back at her with hollow eyes and a slack jaw. His twitching fingers were the only remaining sign of his quickly vanishing life.

Vix crouched down and leaned in close. "You spent my whole life underestimating me. You won't do that anymore."

And she closed her eyes as his last breath gave way. She knew, in the moment that followed, that he was gone and that the vision had bled away. Her heart thumped in her chest, like a wildcat trying to break out of its steel ribcage. She felt no guilt, but instead, *love*. A burning, ferocious love and loyalty for Margo for granting her such a gift. How had Iona been scarred by this process when it was so healing?

"Open your eyes. . . my woman."

So she did. In the darkness, she saw Him. Him, with his broad nosed, deer skull and feminine human hands. His antlers, terrifyingly large and sharp, were adorned with red, stringy material, like flesh, but otherworldly and pulsating—almost like a freshly gored human body. His chest was a mass of coarse hair like a bearskin rug, and his body filled with eyes of varying sizes and shapes. The blood red pupils all seemed to glow.

"What is your name?" Vix asked.

"You know it already."

She nodded. The wisp of a name formed within her mind, but it wouldn't come to her. Yet, the intense familiarity remained, like connecting with an old friend. Perhaps He had always been part of her—it didn't matter. His name was not nearly as important as His presence. He stood in the light of the flame, and suddenly, Vix felt very cold. She watched as puffs of fog leaked from the nostrils of His skull and from between His bony teeth. The flames around them turned almost blue and then pink.

"You did not run," He stated calmly.

Vix shrugged. "I didn't feel the need to. And she told me not to."

When He breathed, she could feel the house shudder around her from the sheer force of it. "What do you seek?"

"To pledge my loyalty to Margo. To have her know I will love her always."

He tilted His head to the side. "Is that right?"

"Yes," Vix said, but she did flinch. And at that, He chuckled.

"Granted. And what of your other wishes?"

"My other. . ." Vix trailed off, completely confused. She didn't think this was a part of the plan. Was He like a genie? Was it a three wishes sort of situation?

He seemed to have heard her thoughts. "I am not a djinn."

"Then what are you?"

"I am neither an angel nor a demon. I am the manifestation of All, beyond what the reaches of your human mind can comprehend." He tossed His head, shaking some of the strings loose from His antlers. They splattered against the floor with a satisfying wet slap. "Be mindful, my woman. You have undertaken the arduous process of coming here, and you can only be here once during your soul's lifetime. Tell me, what else is it that you wish for?" He circled her, and after taking five steps, disappeared into the shadows. All that remained was His voice. "Do you wish for power? Do you wish to be the most beautiful?"

Vix already had power through Margo. And to be the most beautiful was something completely subjective; even she wouldn't wish for something as superfluous as that. But His voice grew taunting, teasing.

"Really? You've struggled to adapt to your new lifestyle. . . you want beauty to not come to you effortlessly? Easily?"

She didn't want to upstage Margo.

"You truly are loyal. You came here to ask me for something you already have, my woman." He stopped, and she knew He was directly behind her. "But I can grant you other things. Grant you things that even she wished for."

"Margo. . . asked you for something else?"

"She did. What if you had the ability to pursue beauty regardless of pain?"

"Beauty regardless of. . ."

"Imagine." His skull-face rested on her shoulder, affectionate and familiar. "If you no longer felt hunger when you didn't eat. You're smart, unlike the previous one who came here."

"Iona?"

"Her wish was that she could indulge in her habits without fear of death. Doesn't mean she won't come close to it and doesn't mean that she doesn't suffer. Sweet woman, but unworthy of this gift, and to share this gift with Margo. So I grant you this suggestion as a token of my fondness for you, as one of the most impressive subjects that has approached me thus far." Vix considered it. The intermittent fasting *was* more than a little frustrating, and on her photoshoot sets, she was so tempted by the assortment of snacks on the crafty table. His soft fingers clamped around her arms, squeezing her tightly. "Yes, yes, isn't it? So it is done. I shall grant you this other gift."

"And my loyalty?"

"She will know you are loyal once you return." He circled around to face her. "Now. Let's drink to it."

Vix was confused. Drink what? Water? Wine? His blood? But no. He touched her face, still red and dripping with her father's fresh blood. He opened His mouth, and from the bottomless depths, a tongue, thick and pink, emerged. He tentatively licked her face, then retracted. A deep moan erupted from the pit of His chest, and she felt His tongue on her face again, licking it off. She felt moved, her body rumbling with desire. She, too, wiped some of the blood off her face, and stuck her fingers in her mouth. She sucked, long and hard, tasting as the bitter iron bled away into sweet, like the Moscato Margo served at weekly dinners.

He watched her like a predator watches His prey. But she felt no fear, because she was equally powerful in this moment. He continued to lick, His tongue smearing the blood around her face. His feminine hands stretched forward and tore at her blouse, and though she was now exposed, she still felt no fear. The grizzled edges of His skull-teeth made their way down her neck, to the center of her chest, and He pulled down her skirt in one swift motion. His fingers stretched inside of her, and she resisted the urge to moan.

"This is how we seal the pact," He told her.

She nodded, her body rumbling. His fingers wrapped in her hair as He pulled her to the ground and spread her legs apart. The blood dripped from His face onto her milky white thighs. The pupils of His many eyes fixed upon her and seemed to burn her skin, but the pain was delicious. He pinned her wrists against the ground, and she did not struggle, for she did not want to. His hands became like claws, gripping onto her and leaving red marks underneath. And then He plunged into her body. At first, it felt searing hot, and she almost screamed from pain—but then it felt good, *sinfully* good, and her screams became that of joy. Her mind became lost, in a torrent of love and pleasure and power, her voice crying out Margo's name. The world faded around her, until she could see nothing but darkness, yet still, the sensations remained, blissful and aggressive in their lust for her.

Vix didn't know when the dream had ended, and when she had reentered reality. All she knew was that she was naked, and her clothes were torn, and a wetness leaked from between her thighs. She touched it—it was hers. Some scratches were on her body that stung, but not too much, and the blood she had bathed in was gone. Bewildered, she sat up, her body sore and aching from acts of pleasure. The chalk tapestry beneath her had scalded from pink to red ash. She knew it hadn't been a dream. She had laid with The Entity.

The door to the basement opened, and Margo came down the stairs with a soft down blanket she had fetched from the living room. She crouched beside Vix and examined her body with wide eyes.

"He. . . wow. He chose you."

"Margo, I. . . I'm sorry. I think I got carried away."

"Why are you apologizing?" Margo's eyes burned brightly, with an excitement that sent Vix's heart a-pounding. She squeezed her hand. "Vix, He chose you. He chose you as He chose me and my mother before me. He only chooses the most powerful women. This is the first time He's chosen someone outside of my lineage."

"Really?"

"That I know of. I don't know who else has summoned Him. He doesn't exactly keep a guest-book." Margo squealed with childlike delight and hugged Vix. "For Him to choose you is like for my family to choose you; like I have their approval."

"So you believe me now? That I'm loyal to you and you alone? And that I love you beyond all else?"

Margo cupped Vix's face in her hands. She squeezed her cheeks together with an almost frightening warmth. Pressed her lips against hers and allowed her the taste of her tongue.

"I do." Margo wrapped her arms around her neck. "I do."

* * *

After taking a shower and dressing for the day, Vix headed into the kitchen. Her hunger pangs were gone, and she eagerly helped herself to a cup of iced coffee. But Margo wagged her finger.

"You don't fast today. You have to eat something. Let me make you egg whites."

She reached into the fridge and withdrew a cardboard container and shook it. Vix sipped her coffee, and with a blissful smile, watched as Margo went to work. No more than two minutes had passed before her phone started vibrating in her pocket. Annoyed, Vix pulled it out so she could send it to voicemail, but then she saw on her caller ID the word, "Mom."

Perplexed, Vix answered it. "Did you get the check I sent you last week?"

The connection was crackly. "Vix?"

"Yeah Mom?" Vix plugged a finger in her ear. "What's going on?"

"I. . . I'm sorry to tell you this, but Randy died this morning."

"Who is—" Then she remembered. Her father. His name was Randy. He had been referred to as "That Rat Bastard" so many times that she had nearly forgotten. "Oh. Oh shit."

"He died from a heart attack." She couldn't tell if the flatness in her mother's tone was from shock, or because she couldn't care less. "Just thought you should know." Another sober pause. "Are you coming back home for the funeral?"

In the following week, Vix returned to Wichita, and attended the funeral hand-in-hand with Margo. It was the sort of sad funeral you would expect for any miserable alcoholic bastard, where his bar buddies would show up not to celebrate his life, but to steal from the snack table at the wake that followed. Margo was charming and gracious to Patty, even when she scowled at her throughout the funeral. Her mother pulled her to the side once the ceremony had ended, and snarled, "I can't believe you brought *her* into a house of God."

Vix slapped her mother's fingers away, and that was that. Gran hung her head in disappointment. Coolly, Vix appraised her.

"Well, till I send the next check in the mail," Vix said, putting on her sunglasses. "I think we're done here."

Patty sighed out of frustration, now docile at the mention of money. "Vix, you can't just—"

"—Margo, we're leaving."

Margo, who had been introducing herself to a few adoring family members, smiled like plastic. She approached Vix and looked at Patty and Gran, nearly towering over them.

"It was lovely to meet you both," Margo said in a monotonically pleasant voice— her passive aggressive Midwestern way of stating that it was, in fact, *not* pleasant to have met them. She placed a hand on Vix's waist and Patty's eyes seemed to burn. But it didn't move Vix at all—only bored her tremendously. She exited the establishment with Margo without another word.

When they returned home, Margo took the liberty of canceling Vix's various modeling appointments and interviews.

"I know you didn't care about your dad," she said, "but you never know how these things will creep up on you. It's best to have you rest."

So had returned the sweet, almost maternal Margo that Vix had fallen in love with when they first met. Doting and caring, tending to her needs at every hour while still looking flawless for the 'gram. Vix hadn't cried once and had ignored her mother's messages and phone calls with a dismissive, "I'm busy," or, occasionally, impersonating her personal assistant. She laid in bed and didn't eat and relished the fact that she no longer felt pain from this, but on occasion, she did allow Margo to feed her.

"I'm glad you're taking your diet seriously, but

it's as I said to you when you first met. Your body's in style." Margo rubbed her thigh. "I know you don't like them, but they are money makers. And when they aren't anymore, we'll get rid of them. I promise."

After a month marinating in the darkness of her bedroom, Vix emerged fresh-faced, but the dark auburn roots of her normal hair color were bleeding in through the stark white blonde. Grimacing, she examined her face in her bathroom mirror with frustration.

Margo watched her from the doorway. "We'll get it redone."

"It's going to take weeks to get it back to what it was before. I can't bleach it all at once, like I did the first time. Remember how that almost made my hair fall out?" Margo nodded. "And I want to get back to work. I need it." Vix sighed, gripping the edges of the counter. "I'm tired of lying in bed all day."

"Well. . ." Margo trailed off. She looked at Vix, her head tilted to the side and lips pressed together in a curious line. "I have an idea. I'm not sure if you'll like it, but. . . you might be able to handle it."

"Handle what?"

"There's this kind of. . . hair transplant procedure that's been making a buzz in the underbelly of the industry." Margo rolled her eyes. "They replace every single hair on your head with the color you want. All natural human hair, and no need to ever redye it. I know that you have such beautiful natural hair, but you could always dye it back, if you wanted."

Vix remembered the gift that The Entity had given her. And she nodded, slowly. "Let's do it."

Five hours later, they arrived at the facility owned by a woman named Consuela Bardal. She was a surgeon, Margo had explained, but she carried the air of a queen. She wore loud pink stripes and tailored slacks, and her skin was impeccably smooth. The only thing that betrayed her age were the small crow's feet at the corners of her eyes. After a brief consultation and the delivery of a check in the amount of $560,643, Vix changed into a medical gown and waited for Consuela to change into her scrubs—also hot pink. She connected her to an IV, and when the sharp needle entered her vein, Vix felt nothing. Sweet, blissful nothing, followed by the release of warm, euphoric drugs. She was wheeled into an operating room with a small viewing chamber, and on the other side of the glass, Margo patiently waited.

"You will feel discomfort," Consuela promised her. "It's a very painful process. At times, you may want to close your eyes. Rest assured, at the end, you will be left with beautiful low maintenance hair."

Consuela used medical grade tweezers, a scalpel, and several syringes full of numbing drugs. Vix could feel the first needle hit the top of her forehead, but felt nothing, and even after it was injected, still. Nothing. Consuela used the tweezers to begin removing the hairs, and Vix could feel the warm blood surface up from the pores and course down the sides of her head. Consuela wiped it away with a small damp cotton pad and started afresh.

"Now, that's just the little baby hairs," Consuela explained to her. "We have to remove the rest."

Consuela's scalpel sliced through the uppermost layer of Vix's skin, like she was an apple to be prepared for a pie. Vix watched as bloody bits and pieces of her scalp went into a plastic tub; the kind you would use to mix cement. Each piece she removed was replaced with synthetic skin, lined with beautiful platinum hairs. And even though she was bleeding, and well aware of the fact she was supposed to be in pain, Vix was not.

And Margo realized this too. Her brow furrowed and she crossed her arms, watching as Vix's scalp and head were torn apart, and as the new platinum white hairs were threaded through. The ten-hour procedure was more exhausting for Consuela, who had to call for a break twice. When it was done, Vix's red, raw head was full of gorgeous, enviable hair.

Vix returned home and spent a few days recovering in bed. Her adoring public awaited her on all of her social media channels. The get-well soons, the we're-so-sorries, the we-love-yous—flooding each and every single comments section, all the way back to some of her oldest posts. With a soft smile, she showed them to Margo.

"We can use these," was all she said.

The next day, Margo came into Vix's room with a script for YouTube. A long, heart-wrenching script talking about her troubled relationship with her late father in the vaguest of terms; the angst and guilt from her remorse laid out in the most down-to-earth of passages, it could've been pulled from a sappy YA novel.

"They care about you, and you need to use that," Margo whispered into her ear. She held Vix's face in her hands. "When we first met, you said you didn't want to be an actress. But can you act?"

"With you here, I can do anything," Vix promised.

So Margo, in tandem with Iona and Lindsey, set up the room, and Vix was sat at her desk. White-bright ring lights framed either side of her, and in her camera, she could see how heavenly she looked, even with her puffy tired eyes—like an angel scorned. Margo applied the makeup, adding dark, smudged lines underneath her eyes, and a satisfied comment, "Sad but sexy." Lindsey tested the mic and camera, and then, they were off. Vix stared into the lens of the DSLR, propped level with her head, and when she looked into its never-ending abyss, she felt nothing. The first few lines of the script, she delivered with a monotone voice. Margo ordered her to start over. "Concentrate. Conviction, babe." Vix squeezed her eyes shut and took a deep breath. When she opened them again, she imagined she was looking directly into Margo's eyes.

"Hi everyone," she said, her voice cracking with a sadness that she didn't know she could feel anymore. "I just wanted to thank you for your well wishes in the wake of my dad's passing. It's been hard for me. As many of you know, my dad and I weren't close. And in a lot of ways, it hurts because there's no way I can bridge that divide between us. He's just. . . gone." The tears bubbled up in the back of her throat at will, and for a moment, Vix wondered if this was how she truly felt. "For those of you who have lost a parent you've been estranged to. . . I think you're the only ones who could understand what this is like. . ."

Once Vix had finished, Margo and the others clapped. Lindsey congratulated her with a warm hug and whisked away the camera to edit the files. Within hours of uploading the video, Vix had made the headlines of every celebrity gossip outlet in the United States. *MODEL VIXEN MORELLO MOURNS THE DEATH OF HER LATE FATHER IN A TOUCHING YOUTUBE TRIBUTE. IT-GIRL VIXEN MORELLO TEARFULLY TALKS ABOUT HER ESTRANGEMENT FROM LATE FATHER. VIXEN MORELLO, SUPER-MODEL MARGO ERIKSEN'S RUMORED LOVER, TALKS ABOUT HER LATE FATHER.* And thereafter came the thoughtful think pieces published by outlets like Bustle and Jezebel. *When Vix Morello talked about her father, I thought about my own. We don't talk enough about parent estrangement. Like Vixen Morello, I too, spent every Father's Day wondering what I did wrong.* It was the most overwhelming outpouring of support and love that Vix had ever received. She lay awake in the dark of Margo's bedroom that night, scrolling through the various articles across social media. Margo, pressed against her side, watched her tenderly and ran her fingers through her soft silver hair.

"When my mother died, this was how they reacted," Margo explained quietly. "All love, all support. I hate to say it, but sometimes, a tragedy is what you need to give your career a little jumpstart. Gives you a cause. Makes you memorable. Besides, better to exploit your own pain than let others do it for you."

"What was your cause?"

"Empowering young women," Margo said with a laugh. "I thought that was obvious. You know I run that foundation, right? GrrlPower United?"

It was one of the many countless things that Margo "did." Vix nodded.

"Well that only started after. . ." Margo shook her head and smiled. "When I was a teenager. I met a very sleazy fashion designer. And he ended up. . . doing what sleazy men do to naive teenage girls whose mothers were too busy drinking in the dressing room to notice. He was over six feet tall, and I didn't stand a chance."

"I'm so sorry."

Margo waved a hand dismissively. Chuckled a little. "Oh, what happened wasn't even the worst of it. The worst was the look on his face afterward when he swaggered out into the photoshoot. Pigheaded, triumphant, like he had won something. I wasn't a prize but a conquest. You know the feeling."

Unfortunately, Vix did.

"Anyways, after that, that's when I did the ritual. With Him. And when I came to the next day, I discovered the designer had died in a car accident. And for some reason, I just. . . felt compelled to come clean. And when I did, it felt like I was in the world's embrace. They couldn't get enough of me. And the jobs came in once again. Then my mother passed when I was twenty-two, and I got my second wind." Margo shook her head. "My point being, Vix, is that humans are leeches. They *love* tragedy. They can't get enough of it. They feel sorry for you, and if you can carry yourself with grace, they will love you all the more for surviving it."

"So. . . not for what I do, but for what I've been through."

"Does it matter?" She arched her brow. "What matters is that, regardless of the reason, they love you. And so you'll keep getting work. And hopefully, one day, you'll have a legacy to pass on."

"You think so?"

Margo laid her head against her chest. She wove her fingers through hers. "I know so."

PART THREE

But even the most sensational, inspirational of stories cannot hope to remain in the public eye for longer than a few months, and so was the case for Vix. Countless interviews, dozens of podcasts, and multiple magazine articles—then stark silence. A quiet return to her eventful modeling career, and her slow ascent to stardom. It shouldn't have come as a surprise to Vix that someone would swoop in to take her place and become the next hot new member of the Bleach Babes, but of course, it did, and it stung like the juices of a bitter fruit on an open wound.

Ji-woo Seong. two hundred thousand followers. Former K-Pop idol who left her tumultuous girl-group to independently pursue her music career as a songwriter—so not only did she have the K-Pop background going for her, she had the serious, indie musician side going for her as well. Her Insta and TikTok had modest numbers until her acoustic cover of the Traveling Earls' *Need to Forget You* went viral on the latter platform, causing her to blow up astronomically. She dyed her hair bleach blonde before she even entered the house and moved into Vix's former bedroom—Vix had long since moved completely into Margo's bed. With a polite smile and the grace of a princess, she had approached Vix on the day of her interview and shook her hand, and Vix had noticed, with a twinge of jealousy, that Jiwoo eerily reminded her of Leilani. They looked nothing alike, but their auras were the same. To be confronted by a person with such a similar background disgusted her.

I had replaced her, Vix thought, the muscles in her jawbones taut with ripe anger, stiffly refusing to smile. *I had replaced Leilani, and now we've got another fucking musician. Great.*

"I'm a big fan," Ji-woo said. "I've been following you since before you were even with the Bleach Babes. I absolutely love your style."

With disdain, Vix noticed that her nails were freshly polished pink. Margo jubilantly approached, her arms wide open for a hug. The two had never met, but they interacted like they had known each other for years. Vix, stewing in jealousy, watched the two chatter, and, as the minutes passed and their giggles intensified, accepted the sinking feeling that she was about to be replaced. Ji-woo had the chef make hotpot for her inaugural weekly dinner, and although Vix and Margo had shared this meal many times before at restaurants like DongHae, Margo marveled over its ingenuity, like she had never eaten it before. Predictably, Iona ate her food with the tiniest, most pitiful bites she could muster. At least, unlike with the burger, she could get away with it— all she had to do was state the broth was too spicy.

Even ketchup was too spicy for Iona.

The day after, Margo wanted to take Ji-woo shopping for new clothing, and Vix insisted on tagging along, even though her lover's watchful blue-eyed stare warned her against it. Margo had addressed her with a sweet smile that was so indifferent to her pain, Vix felt like crying.

"Don't you have someplace to be today?"

"I don't know." Vix shrugged her shoulders. "You usually run my schedule, don't you?"

Margo blinked. With a heavy sigh, she allowed Vix into the backseat of the convertible. Ji-woo rode shotgun, another fact that caused Vix's resentment to simmer more earnestly. When they went shopping that day, she noticed how Margo pointedly ignored her heated stare. It was as if Vix was nothing more than a fly on the wall, and although Ji-woo, polite as she was, kept trying to talk with Vix and engage with her, inevitably Margo would distract her with another sequined skirt or overpriced crop top. At one point, Margo seemed to go *fuck it*. When Ji-woo modeled another outfit for them, she squealed with delight and placed her hands on Ji-woo's tiny, almost nonexistent hips. Her body was rectangular—very smooth lines from her shoulders to the soles of her feet.

"God, I just—I *love* your body," Margo said, her voice a luxurious purr. "It's so easy to dress you, because everything looks good on you."

"Margo, stop!" Ji-woo giggled. "You're a literal supermodel. You're the type of woman who could wear a brown paper bag to a red-carpet event!"

"And you, my dear—you could wear nothing."

At once, Vix's vision seemed to darken. She watched, her hatred broiling in the pit of her stomach, as Ji-woo and Margo fawned over one another. Vix looked down at her plump thighs thick as rotisserie chickens and desperately wished that she could carve into herself and slice away the steaming layers of fat. The Entity had likely given her that power; it wouldn't take much. A few slices here, a severed artery there. She shook her head to get rid of her intrusive thoughts, and instead distracted herself with the comments section of her Insta, filled with messages from her adoring fans. Where she had once felt joy, she now felt only a slight twinkling of excitement; it had faded after the countless months that she had spent interviewing, photographing, and modeling. Not even these hundreds of thousands of people soothed her fears gnawing at the pit of her stomach now.

Only the words of one person could. And when

she crawled into their bed that night, her lips pursed together in a playful pout, Vix pretended that she wasn't as furious as she really was. She traced small circles on Margo's shoulder with the tip of her finger and stared at her longingly. Margo continued to scroll through her phone. Vix felt as though her mouth was full of wet cotton balls. She had to swallow a couple of times before her throat felt moist enough to speak, and even when she did, she still sounded hoarse.

"I thought you liked how *my* body looked."

Margo arched her brow, pointedly annoyed. "Is that what you've been upset about this whole day?"

"You knew I was upset, and you didn't—"

"—Not everything is about you all the time. You made Ji-woo feel uncomfortable." Margo shook her head and turned her attention back to her phone.

"Really? *I* made her uncomfortable? Not you touching her itty-bitty little waist?"

"And what about it? You're acting like I'm some sort of predator."

Hesitation, then: "Maybe you are."

Margo's eyes flashed. She glared at Vix with an untenable ferocity that she had not seen before. Something haunted and full of hatred surfaced in the pitch-black pupils of her eyes. It was borderline otherworldly. But with a deep breath and passive-aggressive shake of her head, it dissipated.

"Jealousy isn't a good look on you."

"Don't give me a reason to be jealous then. The

way you're doting over her now is like how it was when I first moved in here with you—"

"—Oh my God, Vix, you're acting like a total sociopath. I am being nice to someone who is joining the collective, therefore I must be a horrible fucking human being."

"That's not what I'm saying, I'm—"

"—You really think that I have such little respect for you that I would *fuck* another woman in our house?" Margo flung back the covers of the bed. She stood up with a huff and crossed her arms, hovering almost menacingly over Vix. Eyes hard, breathing hard—and in the heat of the red LED lights, they once again seemed almost pitch-black. "You're not a baby, Vixen. You should know how to regulate your emotions by now. That means being an adult and not acting like you've shat your pants the whole day when we're working with someone. All this money, all this success, and you're going to sit there and act like that?"

Vix's eyes blurred with tears. Margo groaned and rolled her eyes. Vix didn't sob, although she wanted to. She swallowed back a lump in her throat and spoke softly.

"I'm not crazy, Margo. I saw how you looked at her. How you touched her. *What you said to her!* And it's—"

"—Stop." Margo held up her hand, her tone of voice flat.

"—Y-you said that you didn't like rectangles,"

Vix blurted out, her voice shrill with desperation. "You liked women with *hourglasses*. She's a box with four perfect corners. She doesn't fit the Bleach Babe brand. Why would you let her in? What, am I not good enough to replace Leilani?"

Margo's eyes widened in shock. She shook her finger at her. "Don't you *dare* mention Leilani to me. Don't you *dare*. As if she could ever be replaced."

"Seems like that's what you're doing. If you want me to pick up a guitar or take some singing lessons, I could. I could do anything you want."

"I'm not going to entertain this discussion anymore. I don't have the time, I don't have the patience, and quite frankly, I don't know where you get the audacity to talk to me like this when I'm the one who has given you so much of your success. We run an organization many would *kill* to be a part of, and Ji-woo worked her ass off to get here. Of course I'm going to give her my undivided time and attention; it's the same that I would give to everyone else."

Vix stared back at her. "You don't touch Iona. Or Greta. Or Lindsey."

Margo didn't flinch, but she did fall silent. Then: "This is moronic." Margo laughed, shaking her head, and in the next instant, she snapped her fingers and pointed towards the door. "Get out."

Now Vix was in tears. Full on sobbing. She stood up, wrapped her robe around her body, and exited the room. She stumbled down the hallway with blurred vision and ignored Lindsey's calls to her. She walked downstairs and into the kitchen, where she helped herself to another glass of rosé—her fifth drink that evening. Standing in the pale moonlight streaming through the window, she thought back to that last day that Dharlyn lived in the house. About how Dharlyn had told her that the level of control wasn't as perfect as it seemed; about how one day, it would seem suffocating. Truth be told, Vix didn't find it as suffocating as it was sad. She gave so much of herself to Margo—fickle, beautiful, bitchy Margo —and like a toddler's toy, she was discarded as soon as something better came along. Another trend to capitalize, another way to make money, another lover who would one day crawl into her bed and whisper sweet nothings into her ear in the red shadows of her bedroom. Maybe it wasn't happening now, but it would happen eventually. Even though she knew this, her heart still yearned for her. Perhaps the pact she made with The Entity had been a stupid one—she pledged her loyalty to Margo but didn't ask for The Entity to have Margo give hers in return.

Such a foolish, foolish wish from such a foolish, foolish girl.

Glass in hand and tears rolling down her cheeks, Vix stumbled out of the kitchen and wandered throughout the house. She entered the bathroom and looked at her body in the mirror. Even on a diet as restrictive as hers, she couldn't help but see herself as an overstuffed Christmas ham with pork sausages for legs. Curves in all the right places but making her body a little too wide. Unfortunately for her, that was no longer on-trend. Why else would Margo have accepted Ji-woo into the fold if she was not beautiful? Now her reflection, her facade, her body: worthless. While Vix still had the money, she lacked the joy. The pure, unbridled joy that she had felt when Margo's hands coursed over her and told her that she was worthy of being a fashion icon.

That she was a God.

If Ji-woo's body was what was in style now, well, Vix could conform. She would have to. It would be the only way to ensure Margo's attention didn't sway elsewhere. She could get herself into that rectangle shape, come hell or high water. Get rid of the roundness of her chin and have that fresh turnip shape that she had.

Vix turned her head to the side in the mirror and pressed her tongue flat against the roof of her mouth, perfectly lifting everything into place. A perfect shape, curved and unswollen, and when she smiled, no lines pulled back to reveal the pockets of bubbly fat. She lowered her tongue and placed it, lowered it and placed it, and soon, she found herself with a wild idea. It was outrageous, but she remembered The Entity's words, the promises that she had made with him—and she knew that no matter how strange it seemed, it would work.

After all, who needed a tongue when you had such a killer smile?

Less than half an hour later and with two more glasses of wine bubbling in her stomach, Vix returned to the bathroom. She checked the time on her phone—3 a.m.. So late that not even Iona would be up and purging the contents of her stomach. She could pursue her task uninterrupted.

She frowned, looking at her expression in the mirror, and then glanced at the floor. Sitting on top of the toilet was a stack of fluffy white towels she had brought into the room. Vix stripped down to her bare skin and threw the towels underneath her feet, then looked at herself once more. She pulled her long, moon-blonde hair into a ponytail and grabbed the other object she had brought into the room.

A stapler from Margo's office.

She unbuckled it so that both ends peeled apart from each other and held it up high like a dagger. She looked at her face in the mirror and pressed her tongue up flat against the roof of her mouth, perfectly nestled just behind her front row of teeth. She opened her mouth as wide as she could while still keeping her tongue pressed. She slowly inserted the stapler and pressed it against the roof of her mouth.

And then punched it in.

There was no pain, but the shock and force of

the stapler piercing through her tongue caused her to cry out in surprise. She stumbled backwards and her grip tightened on the stapler. Inside, she could feel her tongue thrashing from side to side with a ferocious strength, like a wildcat trying to break out of a cage. She could feel the sinews of the muscle pulling apart underneath the staples and the reeking iron taste of blood filling her mouth and overflowing, dripping onto the floor below. The stapler was still stuck to her tongue—she should've gotten something that was industrial grade. But this would suffice if she could just make it hold still. She slowly tore the stapler away, feeling more blood rush into the space. Once she pulled it out, she placed it back in, and administered another staple, and this time, she didn't scream.

Vix coughed when some of the blood seeped into the back of her throat, and she stood there for a moment, arms spread wide in a T-pose, head bent downwards, allowing the blood to leak out of her mouth. Tears burned at the corners of her eyes, but they were involuntary. She felt nothing—at most, there was a burning sensation where the staples had entered the bony roof of her mouth: a three-day-old cat scratch already mending itself together. She didn't know how long she stood there bleeding; she only knew that the stained white towels had changed from pink to red, red, red. And finally, she was able to close her mouth. It felt strange, and when she attempted to talk, her voice was only able to form strangled vowel sounds. But it didn't matter. Inside her mouth were four glittering jewels; a cheaper yet more precious silver that couldn't be found in her jewelry box. Her jawline was smoother than ever—it was a better facelift than any plastic surgeon could perform, because it was hers; it was proof that she was limitless and boundless in her pursuit for beauty. She could be anything and everything, thanks to The Entity. Could reshape herself in any way that she desired.

She could become something that Margo would love again.

And again, and again, and again.

* * *

After cleaning up the bathroom, Vix crept off to the guest bedroom, and she slept there until just before noon. By that time, Margo had taken Ji-woo and left, and their other housemates were busy with work. Vix showered and helped herself to a cup of coffee before going to a photoshoot. She allowed herself to be pampered and doted over, and surprisingly, no one found it strange that she was unable to say a word. Whenever someone asked her a question, she would nod or shake her head, and that was a suffi-cient enough answer. That evening, when she returned home for dinner, she giddily realized that she would no longer be tempted to eat solid foods, as chewing had become next to impossible. All of her temptations—sweets, starches, and cheese-laden carbs—would no longer be an option for her. And even liquid foods would prove a challenge, since she could only drink from a straw and would have to jam that straw in the corner of her cheek to avoid the wriggling, stapled organ.

The next few days passed quite easily, with Vix going to her photoshoots and consuming protein shakes, until Wednesday rolled around, and the house members once again had to meet for dinner. Iona offered Vix a small smile when she came and sat next to her.

"I feel like I haven't seen you in weeks," she said with a laugh. "You've been so busy."

Vix smiled and nodded. She watched as Margo entered the room with Ji-woo. Her gaze flitted to the new girl, who washed her hands in the kitchen sink before taking a seat with the rest of the group. Ji-woo seemed to notice her watching, but she politely smiled and averted her gaze, pretending to engage in the conversation that Greta was having with Lindsey. The chef came to deliver meals that evening: squid and eggplant pesto pasta with cashew parmesan sprinkled atop—and a protein smoothie for Vix. The housemates collectively stared at her as she graciously accepted the drink from the chef, and took a long, loud sip. She noticed with a watchful eye that the chandelier above was beginning to move.

Margo stared at her, and Vix could tell that she

was trying to curb her anger. "You decided to order something else tonight?"

Vix nodded.

"Can I ask why?"

Vix shrugged.

Lindsey wrinkled her nose disdainfully. Ji-woo nervously pushed around some of the food on her plate, watching each member of the house carefully. Vix continued to slurp on her protein shake, blind to the animosity and confusion that was slowly settling over the dinner table like a storm cloud.

"If Vix gets to eat a protein shake, could I have one instead?" Iona pushed back her plate, her voice filled with an unusually loud confidence. "I know I asked the chef to prepare the pasta without the squid, but you never know."

"You will eat every bite of food on your plate and so will she," Margo responded coolly, pointing at Vix with her fork. She waited for a reply, but Vix said nothing. She set down her utensil and calmly folded her hands together. "Why aren't you eating with us? Some sort of dietary restriction I don't know about?"

Vix shrugged.

Lindsey rolled her eyes, annoyed.

"Dude. You can talk, can't you?"

A dark look surfaced in Vix's eyes. She sat there stiffly, her straw pinched between her two fingers. Looks of realization—and horror—emerged in everyone's eyes.

"Vix." Lindsey placed her palms flat on the table. "Vix, say something."

Vix didn't move. The few who had been holding their utensils set them down and leaned across the table. Iona prodded Vix's side with a nervous laugh. The chandelier chattered in its musical voice of glass. That familiar, haunting tin-drone sound returned, trembling underneath Vix's feet. This time, she was not afraid of it. She settled into it, pressing her heels down, embracing it as though it was an extension of her body.

Greta asked, "Vix? Hello? What's the matter? Cat got your tongue?"

"Vixen," Margo said sharply, "open your mouth."

Slowly, Vix stood up and attempted to walk away from the table. Panic broke out behind her, the shrieks of every housemate causing the chandelier to rattle violently overhead.

"Grab her!"

It was Greta who first got to her and grabbed her wrist. Vix wrenched around and dug her fresh red acrylic nails through the soft flesh of her wrist, and Greta pulled away with a surprised yelp. For a moment, they paused in shock, watching as a large wound emerged from the mark Vix had made. It bled profusely, and Greta whimpered, woozy. She reached for a napkin as Vix attempted to make a break for it again.

The tin-drone echoed louder.

Lindsey barreled around the corner and nearly tackled Vix, wrapping her arms about her waist and pulling her from the doorway. Vix's fingers dug into the wooden grooves of the frame, but when Iona came and helped Lindsey wrestled her back, she couldn't stop herself from being pulled back into the dining room. Lindsey pressed Vix against the wall while Iona forcefully held her opposite side. Ji-woo hovered in the background, her eyes wide, and her shoulders shaking. Vix wrestled against her friends' grasp, but they didn't let go. Margo swiftly approached, and grabbed Vix's chin, her fingers pressing on either side of her mouth. She tried to pull her jaw open, but Vix resisted, twisting her head from side to side.

"Vix!" Greta cried out, panicked. "Stop it!"

Vix released a guttural growl, a sound unlike anything she had made before. Margo picked up a dinner knife from the kitchen table and huffed in frustration. She pulled Vix's jaw down once again and wrenched the edge of the knife into her mouth. Lindsey started screaming as the overhead lights started to flicker.

"Margo, stop! You're going to hurt her!"

Margo used the knife like a crowbar and pried Vix's jaw open. When she did, three things happened: first, the slushy remains of the protein shake that couldn't get past Vix's swollen tongue dribbled out of her mouth and onto the floor. The girls, sans Margo, cried out in disgust. Second, a little bit of blood, rancid and black, followed. And third, the horrific stench of rot, like an aged cheese cloth stained with acidic bile. It caused Lindsey to gag and recoil with disgust. Vix, defeated, stared back at Margo with tear-stained eyes. Margo examined Vix's teeth, stained red from her makeshift surgery. She used the flashlight from her phone to stare into Vix's mouth. Her tongue was swollen with pus and irregularly shaped like a mushroom. The staples had started to oxidize and had stained the surrounding flesh a gangrenous green.

"Jesus Christ, Vix!" Iona cried out, horrified.

"What the fuck did she do?!"

"I'm going to be sick!"

"Quiet!" Margo turned back to the table. "Everything on the floor *now*. We gotta lay her down."

Vix screamed, her voice ascending into hysterical screeches as the tin-drone grew in volume, rattling the walls, swinging the chandelier back and forth across the ceiling like a pendulum. She began to kick and punch them as they inched her closer and closer to the table. With a sweep of her arm, Lindsey pushed off all the plates and they shattered on the floor. They heaved Vix onto the table, each girl holding a part of her down. Lindsey called for Ji-woo's help and the tearful girl reluctantly assisted in securing Vix's left arm.

Margo left and returned with a staple remover. She crawled onto the table, on top of Vix's body. Vix wrestled and screamed, tears falling from her eyes.

Margo said nothing, just gritted her teeth and held her jaw firmly in place.

She managed to stick the staple remover in her mouth, and she could feel the tips of the device scraping against the crackled edges of the staples. She glared at Vixen.

"The things I do for you."

And she proceeded to rip out the staples, one after the other.

* * *

It came as no surprise to the disturbed house members that Ji-woo elected to move out less than three days after the incident. The girl had been unable to stop crying and was far too traumatized to be persuaded to stay any longer. Margo's sugary sweet facade evaporated like spoiled milk in the hot sun. She coldly told Ji-woo to remember the NDA that she had signed and bid her no other goodbyes.

Vix spent time recovering in the guest bedroom. A doctor had been summoned to the house for discretion, and she was given a slew of antibiotics, along with sedatives, to speed along the recovery process. The mirror had to be removed from the space, because every time Vix woke up and saw her reflection, she sobbed hysterically over her swollen cheeks and cracked, colorless lips. Her teeth had also been split apart in some ways from the incident, leading to her having unruly gaps—not fashionable, and certainly going to ruin opportunities for future gigs. She would have to have braces to replace them, and she would be lucky if the photographers would let her do a closed-mouth smile in the meantime.

The morning after Ji-woo had moved out, Margo visited Vix for the first time. She remained at a cold distance, her arms crossed, her chin held high. Vix could only stare at her from the bed, her body a wrinkled and useless lump in a tangled mess of ten thousand thread count sheets.

"How sober are you right now?" Margo asked.

"I haven't been drinking, if that's what you're asking." Vix's voice was hoarse as she spoke. She cracked a smile.

"Very funny." It wasn't. "The doctor said that he gave you a sedative before he left. How much can you understand right now?"

"I understand you perfectly. Just a little tired."

"Good." Margo shuffled in place. "Ji-woo left. As I'm sure you know."

"Hard not to hear the moving truck."

"Yes, well. . ." Margo trailed off. She shook her head and looked positively dumbfounded. "For the love of God—"

"—there is no God here. Not in this house."

A dark look surfaced in Margo's eyes. She spoke slowly, intensely. "Give me one good reason not to institutionalize you."

"Institutionalize?"

"You need *help*. No sane person would do that to

themselves and carry on like—like nothing was *wrong*. Like they weren't in pain."

Margo averted her eyes. It was so uncharacteristic of her that at first, Vix was confused. And when the realization hit her, she felt her body electrify with anger. Mustering her strength, she sat up, locking her arms around her knees for balance.

"You know."

"What?"

"You. Know," Vix repeated slowly, her hoarse voice giving way to a series of cackles. Margo could only stare back at her in shock and disgust. When Vix could finally quiet herself and wipe the spittle off her mouth, she looked at Margo again with a fierce intensity. "You know that He gave me your gift. And you couldn't stand it."

Margo stared back with cold eyes, but her voice feigned innocence. "I don't know what you're talking about."

"You know *damn well* what I'm talking about, Margo. Do not play dumb with me." Vix ran her hands through her hair and her vision blurred with tears. Passionate feelings of love—and hate—broiled and bubbled inside of her, threatening to spill out from every pore in her body. She looked at Margo angrily, the bitter tears dripping down her cheeks. "He gave me what He gave to you. So that we could be bonded together forever. I did it because I loved you—and that *pisses* you off?"

Margo said nothing.

"How long have you known? Was it the morning I woke up?" Her eyes widened again. "No. It was when I got my hair replaced. Wasn't it? That's why you've been pulling away from me?"

"Why are you so obsessed with me? What I think, what I do, how I react to everything that goes on in your life?"

"Obsessed—" Vix recoiled, both in anger and in disgust. "To love you is to be obsessed with you? Do you even hear yourself right now?"

"You don't love me," Margo snapped. "You took the gift that He gave me. You don't love me; you want to replace me."

"*You* want to replace *me!*" Vix screeched. "That's why you brought her into this house!"

"Why would you take my gift, Vix? What other reason could you have for taking it, other than you want to *surpass me and take over?*" Margo's fists shook with rage. "I brought you in here to be my apprentice, not to overthrow me. To rule by my side —so why in God's name would you ask for a gift that was *mine* to have?"

"He told me you would like it! He acted like it was supposed to be—be a gift! Flattery! I don't fucking know! I wasn't about to argue with a demon in the basement, which *you* left me alone with!"

"You *wanted* to do the ritual!"

"I wanted you to love me!" Vix screamed, her voice breaking into sobs. She looked at Margo, now almost a stranger to her. "I did it to prove myself to you. That was the *only* reason I did that. I don't care about the gift, Margo, I care about you. I love you. I love you so much to the point that I would mutilate myself, over and over, to shape myself into the image of something you would love in return. How can you be so cold?"

Margo came over. She sat down on the bed, her lips in a firm line. She spoke slowly, her hands folded pristinely in her lap. Her eyes remained focused on the ruched lines of her skirt.

"Do you remember what happened when you first came here? What I told you?"

"You told me many things—"

"—Then you're a fool. Because the one thing that I *told* you not to do—the most important thing I told you not to do—was to not fawn over me. To become the snake. And here you are again, a little yearling, incapable of standing on her own two feet without bleating for her mother to come and give her attention." Margo looked at her, her expression cold. "You can staple your tongue. You can cut apart your body. You can tear out your own hair, strand by strand. But for as much as you try, and as much as I adore you, you will *never* be what I want you to become. It's not in your nature."

"Stop with the mind games for five seconds," Vix snapped, throwing her hands in the air. Her body was trembling uncontrollably, but her voice was stern. "Are you saying you don't love me?"

A deep breath. Then, "I could never love you. I never told you that I did, either."

Vix felt as if she was underwater. Her vision blurred, and her airways constricted, and every noise felt both amplified and far away. She sat in the bed, her fingers gripping the edges of the sheets, shaking as Margo's voice faded in and out of focus.

"So. . . for that reason. . ."

A deep breath ran shallow.

"I think. . . it's best. . . that you. . . leave. . ."

Vix struggled to concentrate.

"We can go to the bank. . . find you a place. . . I'll help you. . ."

Vix's eyes darted around wildly. And in her panic, she saw it. A syringe, left by the doctor on the house call.

"You can. . . still. . . be a member. . . but you must be. . . distant. . . from now on. . ."

With Margo's voice echoing in her ears, Vix reached for the syringe. She snatched it off the nightstand and plunged the needle into Margo's arm, but Margo did not scream. She recoiled, but too slowly for Vix, who pressed down on the plunger and injected the sedative into her body. Slurring her words, Margo stumbled away from Vix, trying to get over to the door before she collapsed. The contents of Margo's purse spilled across the floor.

Exhausted, Vix stood and walked to where her lover lay writhing on the ground. The house vibrated beneath her feet as she stalked over, its metallic sound pulsing in her ears like the beat of a drum. Margo had landed facing forward, which had forced the syringe to pierce through her arm. Shards of glass from the device glittered on the surface of the floor below her body. Margo turned her head to the side, her eyelids sleepy, but her pupils wide with shock. Vix collapsed at her side, running her hands through that perfect, gorgeous blond hair. The smell of roses wafted from her perfect scalp. She stroked her head the way a curious toddler would pet a feisty cat. Through gritted teeth, Margo attempted to order Vix to stop—*stop*—but her voice came out in garbled whispers, as strange and foreign as the spell she had cast in the basement so long ago. All at once, Vix felt the eyes of many upon her in the room, though she saw no one.

"I only ever felt beautiful when you looked at me," Vix whispered. She curled up beside her on the ground in a fetal position, her body facing Margo's. It was like they were together in their bed again. "And I felt no pain in pursuing that beauty, except now. You have forsaken me, but that's alright. It's as you said. We are Sisters. We are bonded by Him. He would want us to be together, and who are we to defy Him?"

Yellow drool dripped from the edges of Margo's pristine lips. She struggled to retain consciousness. After several moments of struggling, she was able to speak.

"Vix. . . you can't. . ." she whispered, straining to

get off the floor. She collapsed almost instanta-neously. "Vix, it's the drugs. The drugs are. . ."

". . .Making me see clearly," Vix whispered. "He wouldn't want us to pull apart from one another, Margo. We have to stay together. Stay together forever. As the two beautiful souls we are."

Margo wriggled against the ground, her mouth open, her eyes flickering. Vix touched the carpet beside her wounded arm and found that it was bleeding. Vix, sleepy yet somehow more alive than she had ever felt in her life, reached for some of the contents of Margo's purse. She grabbed her phone and opened it up, then turned it to silent. She fumbled through Margo's music app and selected the perfect song.

I need to forget you
But I don't know why
Each step further I take, the more I want to die
Torn apart inside

Vix fumbled through more of Margo's purse. In it, she found a lighter. She slid her thumb across the ignition and sparks sprinkled the floor like fallen stars. She flicked it again and the flame sputtered to life. Her head reeling, Margo watched Vix through ocean eyes.

Barely awake, I'm barely alive
All of my soul wants to cry, cry for you baby

But my voice comes out in a whisper,
And as I watch you kiss her,
I want to forget you more each time.

When Vix used the lighter to torch the curtain, Margo got a second wind. Groaning, she caterpillar-wriggled her way across the floor towards the door, trying to escape. But Vix, her body heavy, pressed her down against the carpet, and pulled her close, enveloping them in a cocoon. Sobbing, Margo watched as the silky curtain began to shrink and crinkle into black streaks of ash, and the voracious flames migrated over to the floral wallpaper, and the carpet began to burn.

"Maybe you're right, Margo. I could never be the snake. I am that Bambi-faced bitch you accused me of being. But even little fawns shouldn't be underestimated. Because one day?" Vix's voice descended into a raspy, voracious purr. "They might just grow their horns."

Forged in the fires of hell, forged in the bonds of eternity. Ashes to ashes. Dust to dust. And lonely electric heart after electric heart on two separate Instagram in-memoriam posts.

ACKNOWLEDGMENTS

I began writing Mewing in October of 2021. Around this time, I was still in grad school, finishing up the final requirements for my MFA. My thesis film, Serotonin, was a short horror film which focused on a teenager with body dysmorphia and body image issues, things I've struggled with for most of my life.

While I was passionate about Serotonin, given that it was produced in a school environment, there are things I omitted or had to otherwise simplify due to time and budget constraints. After I finished this film, I wanted to explore these subjects even more, just from the angle of the influencer instead. In the influencer-era, there are so many interesting things to unpack—the problematic commodification of identities and tragedies, ever-evolving and rapidly changing beauty standards, and the predatory voices you'll encounter within these spaces. Since I was only working on paper, the sky was the limit. I could make Mewing as weird and disturbed as I wanted it to be without sacrifice, and for that reason, it's been a cathartic project. This subject is so complex, and I've only captured a tiny, chaotic sliver of it, but I hope you'll find I've done it well.

The journey to publication has been a long and challenging one, and I wouldn't be here without the help of several individuals. First off, a warm and wondrous thank you to Alan Lastufka for taking a chance on this bizarre manuscript, and for helping it reach its fullest potential. It has been a privilege and joy to work with you and the others at Shortwave Publishing. Thank you to Nicole for the amazing artwork you created for the preorder campaign; I'm forever in awe of how perfectly you captured Margo and Vix. Thank you to Alex Woodroe for your help on the earlier drafts of the manuscript. Thank you to Bri, Aurora, Cody, and my family as well, for all your love and support.

Finally, thank you to the reader for giving this book a chance.

ABOUT THE AUTHOR

Minnesota native **Chloe Spencer** is an award winning author, indie gamedev, and filmmaker. She is the author of *Monstersona*, *Duality*, and the upcoming YA paranormal mystery-romance *Haunting Melody* and adult horror novella, *Vicarious*. In her spare time she enjoys playing video games, trying her best at Pilates, and cuddling with her cats. She holds a BA in Journalism from the University of Oregon and an MFA in Film and Television from SCAD Atlanta.

chloespenceronline.com

A NOTE FROM
SHORTWAVE PUBLISHING

Thank you for reading ! If you enjoyed *Mewing*,
please consider writing a review. Reviews help
readers find more titles they may enjoy, and that
helps us continue to publish titles like this.
For more Shortwave titles, visit us online...

OUR WEBSITE
shortwavepublishing.com

SOCIAL MEDIA
@ShortwaveBooks

EMAIL US
contact@shortwavepublishing.com

CONTENT WARNING

This book includes depictions of self-harm/bodily mutilation, eating disorders, fatphobia, and minor ableism in dialogue. There are additional instances, or at least implications, that they are treating character identities (such as race, ethnicity, and class status) as commodities. It also includes murder, gore, multiple sex scenes, and brief mentions of sexual assault. Additionally, the story centers on the depiction of an abusive, controlling relationship, which is not meant to be romanticized in any way.